The
Food of Love

The
Food of Love

and
Other Tales of
Lovers, Dreamers
and
Schemers

Melvyn Chase

SUNSTONE PRESS
SANTA FE

Sunstone books may be purchased for educational, business, or sales promotional use.
For information please write: Special Markets Department, Sunstone Press,
P.O. Box 2321, Santa Fe, New Mexico 87504-2321.

Book and Cover design › Vicki Ahl
Body typeface › Baskerville
Printed on acid-free paper
∞
eBook 978-1-61139-283-8

Library of Congress Cataloging-in-Publication Data

Chase, Melvyn, 1938-
   [Short stories. Selections]
   The food of love and other tales of lovers, dreamers and schemers / by Melvyn Chase.
      pages cm
   ISBN 978-1-63293-007-1 (softcover : alk. paper)
   I. Title.
   PS3603.H3794A6 2014
   813'.6–dc23

                              2014018822

WWW.SUNSTONEPRESS.COM
SUNSTONE PRESS / POST OFFICE BOX 2321 / SANTA FE, NM 87504-2321 /USA
(505) 988-4418 / ORDERS ONLY (800) 243-5644 / FAX (505) 988-1025

To Jim, with affection and gratitude

Contents

The McKenzie Harvest

*The natural flights of the human mind are not from
pleasure to pleasure, but from hope to hope.*
—Samuel Johnson

I.

That night, the final selection Katherine McKenzie played was Chopin's E Major Etude, *Tristesse*. It did sadden her, but not just because of its tender, reflective mood. This was Jeremy's favorite piece—Jeremy Greene, her fiancé, who was a second lieutenant in General Pershing's army, "somewhere in France," as the newspapers put it.

Katherine paused a moment, setting aside Jeremy's image, her memories of their time together, so she could focus on the music. She breathed deeply, an indrawn sigh, arched her hands over the keyboard and began.

She was tall, slim, her honeyblond hair gathered in a low, loose bun. Her fingers were long and slender, her movements so subtle that the piano seemed to be playing itself, responding to her caresses.

The audience was some thirty of her colleagues at the Fielding Academy for Women, a private secondary school. They sat in a reverent semicircle around her, filling the school's music room. The windows opposite the piano looked out at the neat row houses of Boston's Beacon Street. The leaves of the Academy's massive oak tree trembled in the warm summer breeze off the Charles River, as if it were sharing in the sadness.

As the last echoes of the Etude died away, the audience applauded hesitantly, then more vigorously as Katherine stood up and bowed her head.

"Brava!" That was the Headmaster, Julius Bratton, and others echoed the word, adding "Beautiful," "Lovely."

"Thank you," Katherine said, blushing. "Thank you so much."

A few minutes later, as they were having coffee in the parlor, Bratton said, "I know I'm just repeating myself, and perhaps I should mind my own business..."

Katherine interrupted. "I appreciate the offer, Julius, but it would be a mistake."

"It's worth a try."

She shook her head.

"When I was twenty, just out of the Conservatory," she said, "I thought I was ready. I wasn't."

"You were too young."

"Three or four years ago—again, it was no better."

"You play so beautifully."

"For colleagues. Friends."

"Just pretend the audience is *two hundred* colleagues and friends."

Katherine smiled.

"It doesn't work that way."

"Maybe it could."

She shook her head.

"Why not talk to Brian?" Julius said. "Play for him? An audience of one."

"What kind of client would I be? I'd just let him down."

"You're older now."

"But not ready."

"Are you sure?"

She smiled and nodded.

"Don't get me wrong, Kathy. You're a wonderful teacher. A treasure."

"I suppose this is the time to ask you for a raise."

"It's the time to start a concert career."

"I'm happy teaching."

"Yes, but..."

"Ask me again on my thirtieth birthday."

"More opportunities lost."

"I'll be a married lady by then," she said. "Maybe even a mother."

"If you need someone to watch your children while you concertize—I might volunteer to do it."

She laughed. "I'll make a note of that!"

Later that night, after midnight, Katherine was still awake. She sat at the window of her room on the top floor of the four-story Women's Residence, a few doors down from the main building.

She was one of two unmarried women teachers who lived with the girls to keep a chaperone's eye on them. Nell Coogan, the French teacher, was the other.

The girls were afraid of Nell, and for good reason. She was a tense, easily-angered fifty-year-old, who suspected the worst of everyone, including herself. She was delighted to serve as both judge and jury, and her version of justice was devoid of mercy.

Katherine would much rather forgive and forget. Outside of her classroom, away from her music, she was soft-spoken and shy. And most of the girls, despite their youth and impatience, behaved a little better because they didn't want to upset her.

Tonight, in the silent hours, Katherine sat by the window in the darkness, thinking about her recital and Julius Bratton's offer.

Would it be different if I tried again? Maybe when Jeremy comes back...

Katherine switched on the floor lamp that stood beside her chair. She was holding Jeremy's most recent letter. She unfolded it and read it again.

May 29, 1918
My Dearest Kathy,

We're about to move out. This war. Madness. Impossible to understand. They said we'd stay together. They lied. They've attached my division to the French army. I'm supposed to lead my men, but I don't know how.

Screams all around us, our men, their men, dying. We dig into the mud, we hide in the mud. Men die all around us. We never see the enemy. Guns bark, shells explode, men die. The machine guns cut men down, tear them apart. Why am I still alive?

I try to remember you, my darling. I try, but all I can think about is staying alive. The past is like a dream.

I wish...

I have to go.

I Love You.

Jeremy

Katherine pressed the letter against her breast. She was crying softly. *He loves me. He forgives me.*

She switched off the lamp, lay down in her bed and, after a time, the silence and the darkness soothed her to sleep.

The next morning in the dining room, there were only three for breakfast, Katherine and Nell and the cook, Mrs. Abercrombie, who lived on the first floor of the Residence. The students had left a few days ago—the first week in June—for Newport or Cape Cod and the sundry pleasures their parents' wealth could offer, even in wartime.

Katherine's recital was the final faculty event of the Spring semester. The Headmaster and his wife would spend much of the summer at their cottage on Cape Cod. None of the other staff members lived at the school, except for Malcolm Ryan, the handyman/custodian: he and his wife shared an apartment in the main building of the Academy.

"It's so empty without the girls," Katherine said.

"So *quiet*, you mean," Nell said.

"I love the sound of 'em." That was Mrs. Abercrombie, a sixtyish lady, whose figure proclaimed her approval of her own cooking.

"I do, too," Katherine agreed.

"They make me feel young again," added Mrs. Abercrombie.

Nell shrugged off the idea.

"I was never young that way," she said. "Pampered. Spoiled."

"They're not so bad," the cook said.

"When they're home," Nell wondered, "do you think they'll stick to Meatless Tuesdays and Wheatless Wednesdays?"

"I do," the cook replied. "They love our country, too. And didn't their brothers—lots of them—join up?"

"Many did," Katherine whispered.

"Ready to die for us," Mrs. Abercrombie declared.

Nell changed the subject: "I'm staying with my sister and her family again this summer. In Maine."

"You enjoy that, don't you?" Katherine said.

"For some reason, they keep inviting me back."

"They have two young girls, don't they? Are you really getting away from all this?"

Nell smiled. "They're thirteen and sixteen. But very, very well behaved."

"When *you're* around, I don't doubt it!" Katherine said.

Mrs. Abercrombie laughed.

Nell poured herself a second cup of coffee, added sugar and cream and asked Katherine, "Have *you* thought about going home?"

"I keep in touch. I write to my brother every month or so. I went back—for my mother's funeral. And my father's. I've visited since, once or twice. But I wasn't really at home there. I left so long ago."

"Where was your home?" Mrs. Abercrombie asked. She knew a little about Katherine's origins and, this morning, she felt bold enough to dig deeper.

"Kansas. Haywood, Kansas. In the middle of the state."

"How old were you when you left?"

"Twelve."

"Your mother let you go?" Mrs. Abercrombie wondered aloud. "Kansas is a million miles from here."

"She wanted me to come to Boston. To study."

Mrs. Abercrombie was unconvinced. "There was no place closer to home?"

"St. Louis, I suppose."

"And why not St. Louis?"

"Mrs. Abercrombie..." Nell tried to end the discussion.

"That's all right, Nell," Katherine said. "My mother grew up here. An old friend of hers is a dean at the Conservatory. If I could win a scholarship... Otherwise, we couldn't afford it."

"Indeed," Mrs. Abercrombie said, pursing her lips in disapproval.

Katherine added, "This is where my life is now. My friends. This is where I met my—where I met Jeremy."

"I pray for him," Mrs. Abercrombie said softly.

"We all do," Nell said.

That afternoon, Katherine sat at the piano in the music room playing a few bars tentatively, replaying them with a nuanced difference, then playing them again. At intervals, when satisfied, she picked up a pen that lay on the music shelf and filled in notes on a sheet of staff paper that was propped up on the shelf.

A short, stocky young woman carrying a violin case entered the room briskly, then stopped for a moment or two to listen.

"Hello, Kathy," she said.

Katherine turned and smiled. "Hello, Louise. How are you?"

Louise Warner had been Katherine's classmate at the New England Conservatory of Music and was now teaching there. She also played second violin in the Plymouth String Quartet, a popular Boston ensemble.

Louise kissed Katherine on the cheek, sat down in a chair next to the piano, and pulled a music stand closer. She pushed back a strand of red hair from her eyes and opened her violin case.

"Have you heard anything more from Jeremy?" she asked.

"I have. It's awful there."

Louise took out her violin and bow.

"I know it sounds selfish," she said, "but I thank God that Andrew can't go."

Her husband Andrew was a violist with the Boston Symphony Orchestra. A childhood attack of polio had permanently damaged his left leg.

"I understand," Katherine said.

She played an "A" on the piano once, twice, three times as Louise tuned the A string on her violin, then adjusted the other strings.

"Have they found a new maestro yet?" Katherine asked.

"No. Andrew's quite upset. Who can believe what they're saying about Muck?"

In March, in a storm of war fever, the German conductor of the Boston Symphony Orchestra, Karl Muck, had been arrested and charged as an "enemy alien". Some of the German-American musicians, under pressure, were leaving the orchestra. And a few non-German-Americans, too, in protest. The concertmaster had become the orchestra's new temporary maestro.

"Andrew says they might ask Monteux to help out—to open next season. Until they find a replacement."

"The war touches everything."

Louise sighed and asked, "Have you finished the first movement?"

"I think so."

"Are you satisfied with it?"

"For now."

She put a slim packet of pages on the stand in front of Louise and another on the piano's music shelf.

Louise studied the first page, then spent an intense minute or two on each of the subsequent pages. Katherine waited until Louise turned back to the first page and signaled that she was ready.

Katherine took a deep breath and began to play the minor-key opening of her *Sonata for Piano and Violin*. The tone was a trifle somber, romantic, with passing dissonances that darkened the mood. Louise's violin entered abruptly, attacking the first theme vigorously, aggressively. It was as if the two instruments were pitted against each other, fighting for control. The battle continued until a sudden rest, and a swerve into the softer, lyrical second theme, lightly touched by the piano, caressed by the violin.

Katherine stopped playing, raising her hand.

"I haven't marked it yet," she said, "but you should attack it a little more dramatically. Lightly, but *con brio*. With more spirit."

"We're still in a tug-of-war?"

"Yes."

They replayed the second theme and then passed it back and forth between them.

The tension escalated in the development section of the movement as the two themes were rhythmically condensed, then stretched, passing from minor to major and back again.

The finale didn't quite settle the argument, but reconciled the two themes to each other and interwove them, as the piano championed the first theme and the violin embraced the second.

When they had finished, Katherine said, "What do you think?"

"It's the best thing you've done."

"I'm making some headway with the *Andante*. It's taking shape."

Louise replaced her violin and bow in the case. "I'm looking forward to it."

Katherine smiled. "I don't have any illusions about myself."

"Then you're the only one in the world who doesn't."

"I mean—as a composer."

"I like your work."

"Thank you." She paused for a moment. "You know why I enjoy composing?"

"Why?"

"Everything is so jumbled these days. Nothing seems normal anymore."

She touched the keys of the piano lightly, too lightly to make a sound.

"But music has form. Predictability. That's comforting."

"It's dependable."

"Right."

"In that case, I have a suggestion," Louise said.

"A suggestion?"

"We're planning to do the Schumann *Quintet* in the Fall. We'd like you to join us. One appearance. Just one."

"Louise..."

"Please, Kathy. Do I have to suffer more of *Henry Krauss*? Good Lord!" Katherine laughed.

"He doesn't have half the talent you have," Louise added.

"I can't..."

"Don't answer me now. Think about it."

"Louise..."

"Think about it. Please?"

"All right."

Louise stood up and said, "I'm hungry. The Newbury Tea Room?"

"It's Friday. They'll be serving those *delicious* blueberry scones."

"Let's go!"

II.

On Sunday afternoons when Katherine and Jeremy had begun dating, she was sometimes invited to dinner with Jeremy's family at their Louisburg Square home on Beacon Hill. These Sunday dinners had become mandatory when she and Jeremy were engaged and, after he had shipped overseas, his parents dutifully kept an open invitation for her. The Greenes had decided to stay in Boston this summer, so Katherine knew where she would be spending every Sunday afternoon.

Amos Greene, Jeremy's father, was a successful lawyer with a J.D. from Harvard Law School, an inherited fortune, and a wife, Joanna, who had added her own substantial portfolio of investments to the family's coffers.

The Sunday after Katherine's recital was a dreary, humid day. She left the Residence at one-thirty in the afternoon and followed Beacon Street for several blocks, passing the Public Garden on the way. A quiet stroll along the flower-bordered, tree-shaded paths beckoned to her, but she kept walking to Charles Street, then followed that street up Beacon Hill.

She was wearing her best white cotton summer dress—ankle-length, high-waisted—fashionable, but seen too many times by the Greenes, clear evidence of her limited wardrobe.

Jeremy's seventeen-year-old brother, Jamie, met Katherine at the door.

"I told Wesley" (the butler) "I was taking over this afternoon," Jamie said, kissing Katherine on the cheek.

"What an honor!"

Jamie was awkwardly tall, his arms and legs still unsure of themselves. His thick, dark hair was brush-resistant and his skin was suffering from a surge of hormones. But he was a gentle, affectionate breeze in a home where the windows were shut tight to keep out the rest of the world.

The ritual of dinner was always preceded by a glass of Amontillado sherry in the library. This was Joanna's favorite room, but not because of her taste in literature. True, she prided herself on her collection of rare books, but owning them was far more important to her than reading them. (Jamie had read many of them.)

Her husband had his own library in the den, but it was decidedly pragmatic: books of and about the law.

Jamie led Katherine to the library where his parents were seated in armchairs on either side of a small table with a tray and a bottle of wine between them.

Amos stood up and extended his hand.

"Kathy, my dear. How are you?"

He was a solid, square-boned man, who walked with a heavy step. Just past his fiftieth birthday, his skin was unwrinkled, but his waist was beginning to soften.

She shook his hand, leaned forward and kissed him lightly on the cheek.

"Hello, Mr. Greene."

Katherine walked over to Joanna, who had remained seated, and kissed her on the cheek.

"My dear," Joanna said, without warmth.

She was slim, almost wispy, her faded brown hair styled in loose curls that softened the taut lines of her face.

Amos invited Katherine to be seated. He stood beside her.

"I told Wesley to take to the hills this afternoon," Jamie boasted. "I'm pouring."

Katherine smiled.

"Is that the way you and your friends talk?" Joanna asked.

Jamie blushed.

"Sometimes," he said.

"Not at home, please," Amos said.

After Jamie poured a glass for each of them, Amos raised his and toasted, "To our Jeremy, whom we all love. May he return safely."

He spoke carefully, solemnly, as if every word were being transcribed by a court reporter.

"To Jeremy."

"I was so impressed with his last letter," Amos said.

"Do you get the same feeling? From his letters?" Joanna asked Katherine.

"Well..."

"He's a born leader," Amos interrupted. "Forging a special bond with his men."

"He says they call him Lieutenant Harvard," Jamie said. "And they mean it in a nice way."

"How they must admire him!" Joanna said.

"Yes, of course," Katherine agreed.

"Never a word of fear or doubt," Amos said.

"Never," Katherine repeated softly.

"It's true, we didn't want him to enlist," Amos said.

"Neither did I," Katherine added, her voice trailing off.

Amos and Joanna exchanged a quick glance that Katherine didn't miss.

"But we're very proud of him," Amos said.

"Very proud," Joanna echoed.

Katherine nodded.

They drank their wine in a silence that lasted a moment too long.

"What are your plans for the summer?" Amos asked.

"It'll be a *working* summer. I have lesson plans to develop. I have to select the program for our choir's Christmas Concert. And our chamber orchestra's Spring Gala. And of course, I practice three—sometimes four hours a day."

"Every day?" Jamie asked.

"You have to do the work or you lose ground."

"Discipline," Amos said, with conviction.

"I'm also writing a piece for piano and violin."

"I didn't know you wrote music," Jamie said.

"Neither did we," Joanna said.

"When I was studying...I haven't written anything for a few years. But I felt the need..."

Joanna leaned forward and touched Katherine's arm.

"I understand," Joanna said, "with Jeremy far away."

"Yes, it does help to think about other things."

"Will we ever hear it?" Jamie asked.

"Perhaps..."

"All work and no play?" Amos wondered.

Katherine smiled.

"I have friends. One in particular, Louise Warner. I went to school with her. We go to the movies sometimes."

"Movies?" Joanna said.

"They can be fun," Katherine said. "The Exeter Theatre is just a few blocks away. Charlie Chaplin. The Gish Sisters. Mary Pickford."

The Greenes clearly didn't share her enthusiasm.

"And concerts, of course," Katherine added.

Joanna nodded approvingly. "Of course."

"On Thursday nights," Katherine continued, "we often gather—a group of musicians we know—at Simon Levin's house. You know Simon Levin, the pianist?"

"We've seen him. With the Boston Symphony," Amos said.

"A great talent," Katherine said.

"He's Jewish, isn't he?" Joanna asked.

"Yes, he is." She waited a moment, then added, "Simon calls these gatherings '*musicales*.' We play, listen, argue. Hear the latest gossip. Sometimes a writer joins us. She may read something she's written."

"So we shan't worry about you?" Amos said.

"Please don't," Katherine said. "And I always have my Sundays with *you* to look forward to."

When Simon Levin was a fifteen-year-old Austrian *wunderkind*, he publicly (and, many felt, prematurely) proclaimed his esthetic manifesto: "The greatest music—Bach, Mozart, Beethoven, Brahms, Wagner—blends discipline and romance, tradition and modernity, intellect and passion."

This statement offended Eduard Hanslick, the powerful Viennese critic who believed that emotions have no place in music, that the true beauty of music is its intellectual content, its form and structure. And that Brahms composed "pure" music, while Wagner, Bruckner and the other "modernists" led music astray.

Simon Levin didn't pay much attention to Hanslick, or any other critic. In fact, he never read reviews of his performances—not in Vienna, not in London or Paris, or in Boston, where he settled at the turn of the century. And now, at forty-eight, he was still committed to his youthful manifesto. And he was still astounding the critics, as well as his audiences.

Levin's mansion on Commonwealth Avenue was a perfect reflection of its owner's eclecticism. The furnishings ranged, haphazardly but pleasantly, from elegant to garish. The walls were covered with paintings hung in the European fashion, in tight rows three or four high. Stolid Dutch portraits and pious medieval art were displayed side-by-side with Cezanne landscapes and Impressionist American canvasses—by Childe Hassam and Robert Henri—from the New York Armory Show. Somehow the paintings seemed to harmonize with each other.

Levin's third wife, Helen, was an assertive, Brooklyn-born sculptor, ten years his junior. When the new Museum of Fine Arts had opened in 1909, she was commissioned to create a bust of Levin for the atrium. By the time it was finished, they were engaged. Their accents, hard-edged New York versus a touch of throaty Viennese, created a pleasant tension, a robust fugue for voices.

Levin's maid was a dark-haired, dark-eyed young gypsy from Romania. Her husband was the cook. Occasionally, Levin would invite them to dance as he sang and played passionate gypsy melodies. They were far more dedicated to dancing than to domestic chores, but so were the Levins.

On this Thursday night, there was a special treat at the *musicale*: Simon Levin played Beethoven's *Hammerklavier Sonata* with a remarkable blend of bravura and melancholy, balancing the inner tensions, offering sentiment without sentimentality, mastering the fugal finale with ease and grace. Levin was relaxed at the keyboard, ignoring one or two missed notes, sometimes humming a fragment of melody.

Katherine immersed herself in his performance, adopting it as her standard, knowing she could never achieve it.

She confessed this to Levin.

"No, no, Katherine, my dear," he said, shaking his head. "You must create your own standards. That was *my Hammerklavier*. I play it differently now than I did a year ago—or twenty years ago—than I will twenty years or perhaps twenty *days* from now."

"Or twenty *minutes* from now," Helen Levin said, and laughed. "You usually surprise everyone, even yourself, don't you, sweetheart?"

Levin smiled. "Do I?"

"Because you play with your heart, not your brain," she said.

"Is that what you do? Is that what we should do?" Louise asked.

Levin looked around him at the musicians, seated in a circle, sipping wine, leaning forward to catch his every word.

"Sometimes," he said. "Tonight, I imagined that poor devil shaping sound from silence, hearing his music only with his soul."

He added, "That may be the best way to play. And the best way to listen."

"I must remember that," Helen said. "For your tombstone."

"Then I'll never rest in peace," Levin said, smiling.

"It's a pleasure hearing Beethoven again," said a young man with a shaggy mane of blonde hair.

"German music is *verboten* these days," Louise observed.

"A foolish species of patriotism," Levin said. "As if Bach or Mozart—"

"Or Karl Muck—" Louise said.

"—Are to blame for the war."

"Some people say this is a 'good war'" the young man said.

Levin frowned. "That's what the winners call them."

Sensing the sudden tension in his audience, Levin added, "I doubt that wars accomplish anything. And chauvinism doesn't suit me."

"I'm a Brooklyn patriot," Helen said, trying to ease the tension. "It's in my blood."

Levin drank some wine, paused for a moment, and said, "I have always been an outsider. Even growing up in Vienna—perhaps because I was an artist at such a young age."

"Talent like yours sets you apart," Katherine said.

"And later, I was truly an outsider, an alien, wherever I lived. Here in Boston, too."

He shrugged.

"I am a Jew, after all—the eternal outsider."

"This is getting too serious for me," Helen said. "I don't want to talk about the war. Or Beethoven's ears. Or my husband's soul."

She scanned the faces around her.

"Deirdre Matthews is here tonight," she said. "Do you have a new poem for us, Deirdre?"

Levin smiled.

"And will it be so—*difficult*," he said, "that no one but Deirdre will understand it?"

Deirdre, an arrogantly *avant-garde*, dark-eyed twenty-five-year-old, shrugged off the comment and said, "I have a poem."

She stepped forward, and clasped her hands tightly in front of her as if she were going to pray. She closed her eyes and in a husky, dramatic voice, began:

> *"Extreme Unction.*
> *"Silver. Shining.*
> *"Thirty pieces.*
> *"Catching sunlight.*
> *"Killing sunbeams.*
> *"Thy Betrayal.*
> *"My Gethsemane.*
> *"Jesu, Jesu..."*

Katherine wandered away from Deirdre's rhythmic chant.

I've always been an outsider, too, she thought.

As a child on the farm, her mother had shielded her from the heavy work.

"We must protect Katherine's hands," she would say.

The other children hated that!

At the Conservatory, for the first time she felt that she belonged. But as graduation approached, when other soloists began to look forward to concert careers, she became an outsider again. A virtuoso who couldn't face an audience. And at the Academy, she knew that her colleagues wondered why she buried her talent in a modest teaching job.

Of course, to Jeremy's parents, she was an outsider—a woman without money or a family name that mattered—with a frail, hot-house talent.

And to Jeremy himself, even to him, on their last night together...

The next afternoon, Katherine was at the piano in the music room of the Academy, in the midst of her exercises, when Malcolm Ryan, the custodian, tentatively edged into her field of vision.

She stopped playing and smiled at him. "Mr. Ryan. What is it?"

"You have a call, Miss McKenzie."

"A call?"

There was one telephone at the Academy, in the parlor. It rarely rang.

"Yes. Mr. Amos Greene."

"Thank you, Mr. Ryan."

Amos? He's never called me before.

Katherine rushed toward the parlor.

Jeremy? My God!

She picked up the telephone receiver.

"Mr. Greene?"

There was no response.

"Mr. Greene? It's Katherine."

"We have—news," he said.

"Jeremy...?"

There was another silence.

"We have—" Amos said, almost too softly to hear, "we have—lost him."

III.

An hour or so after the train left Atchison, Kansas, the endless flat terrain of the Great Plains, baking in the July heat, and the enormous blue-white sky stirred echoes of Katherine's childhood fear—that she would be swept up by an angry wind and carried far, far away from the world she knew.

Her mother had nurtured that fear.

"When your father brought me here, I was afraid," her mother said. "In Boston—those comfortable streets—I felt safe. But here... The sky: angry, brutal. Rainclouds like giant black bugs. Lightning bolts flashing. I wanted to go home. But *this* was my home."

They were at breakfast on a June morning. The rest of the family was out in the fields. It was harvest time.

Katherine's mother was small and slender. Her dark blue eyes glowed with an undercurrent of the fear that had never left her, the fear she fed to her daughter.

"Kansas. A Sioux word. 'South wind.'"

She shook her head.

"Back in ninety-six—you were only four. A terrible year. April and May. Killer tornadoes. More than a hundred people killed."

"In Haywood?"

"No. But not far from here."

She reached out, touched Katherine's face with her fingers and said, "Three or four tornadoes in May, a *family* of them. We were on the edge. I could see one, a twisting thing tearing up the sky. I could feel its breath. I ran with you in my arms, down into the storm cellar. Held you tight."

Her eyes watched that memory.

"They're tall and strong—your father, his son, even his daughters. I could never be that strong. You're like me."

She clasped her thin hands together and said, "This isn't where you belong."

In a few months Katherine was going to Boston.

"You have more talent than me, Kathy. You'll have a better life."

Katherine asked her mother a question she had never asked before.

"Why did you marry Father?"

Her mother remembered: "I was in St. Louis. Cousin Leonard was still alive then. An old, grouchy bachelor. He taught piano, violin. He and your father were cousins, too, by marriage. Leonard had visited us in Boston. He made me promise I would return the visit. I didn't think I would. But a few years later... I was twenty-two. I wasn't sure what to do. I wasn't good enough to be a soloist. I didn't want to teach."

She smiled and added, "And I wasn't impressed with the young men in my life."

Katherine laughed. "You're very pretty. There must have been many of them."

"A few." She frowned. "But even then, I knew you can't count on them. They promise this and that, but they break their promises. Remember, Kathy. Don't let *romance* fool you."

"Did it fool you?"

"I suppose it did. Cousin Leonard got me and your father together. Leonard said your father was in St. Louis looking at new combines. It wasn't true. Leonard confessed that later. He knew your father was lonely. That his wife had died. For three years, he was raising a family alone. He needed help. A wife. Leonard told him about me and invited him to dinner."

"And you fell in love?"

"I had never met anyone like him. So handsome. Tan and strong. Sure of himself." She smiled. "Not like those Boston boys who thought they were God's gift to women."

She paused. The smile disappeared.

"I never imagined how difficult... How could I? How hard the work was. I could cook and clean. Take care of the garden. But I was never able to do my share. After a time, your father accepted that—about me. About you, too."

"And you had music..."

"I came here with a little money. Enough for a down payment on a piano. At least I could make music."

"And I was the only one you taught?"

"Roger, too. The youngest. Seven years old. He was willing to try. He enjoyed it."

"I don't remember him."

"He died when you were a baby. Pneumonia. I think the rest of the family—it was as if he died *because* of the music."

"They didn't really believe that?"

"I think they wanted to."

"Do they love us?"

"Your father loves me. And he loves you. I'm sure of that. But the children... Duncan and Jean Anne were already in their teens. I was only a few years older than Duncan when you were born. Maggie and Roger were still young enough so they were a little easier. It wasn't their fault. But I never felt at home. I couldn't be their mother."

And I couldn't be their sister, Katherine thought, watching the Kansas plain roll slowly past the train window.

But where else can I go?

Second Lieutenant Jeremy Greene was killed near the French town of Cantigny in the first battle fought by American troops in the Great War. He was buried seventy miles northeast of Paris in a cemetery donated by the French government as the final resting place for American servicemen. By Armistice Day, there were 6,012 graves in that cemetery.

"We'll go there someday, when the war is over," Amos Greene said, but Katherine didn't feel that his "we" included her. He and Joanna comforted each other, but they didn't share their grief or their consolation with Katherine. Jamie reached out to her, but his parents gradually withdrew whatever affection they may have felt for Katherine.

She was with them at the memorial service in the Unitarian church on Marlborough Street.

She tried to listen to the Reverend Charles Edward Park, but she couldn't concentrate on what he was saying.

"...Jeremy Greene, a fine, brave young man... in defense of liberty... a man among men... we must learn to know Christ as a man among men, to know Him as a teacher... his soul, bound to other souls, in the light of God's grace..."

The words, the prayers, religion itself meant little to Katherine. For her ever since she was a child, reflecting her mother's feelings, God was as remote and uncaring—and often as cruel—as the Kansas sky.

And whether or not there was a God, she would never have the chance to be for Jeremy what he had wanted her to be.

His last memory of me was empty, without joy.

She knew that Amos and Joanna blamed her for Jeremy's decision to enlist, although she had argued with him against it.

It doesn't matter, she thought. *It's easier for them to blame me than to blame him.*

Before the service was over, she had decided to leave Boston. She didn't know for how long. She had to think about her choices. Her failures. She had to decide what to do next. And she couldn't do that in Boston.

Later that week, she had written to her brother Duncan. She told him about Jeremy's death and asked if she could come back to Haywood.

> *I need time away to make some decisions.*
> *The Headmaster has granted me a leave of absence. He wants me to return. I don't know if I will. But I promise you, I won't stay for long. And I won't be any trouble to you. You know I'm not much use around the farm. But I thought I could give music lessons to the children—or adults—in and around Haywood, earn a little money and help out that way.*

Duncan answered her:

Dear Katherine,

We are all very sorry for your loss. As you know our David is at Aggie school. He's home for the summer. He's 20 and he'll have to register for the draft next year. I hope he can finish school.

You can stay in what we still call the music room. I'll move the couch out and put a bed in. We even kept the piano tuned. Emily tries to play it, not very well.

Don't worry about money. We had a good harvest. Last summer was dry but there was enough snow in the winter and a very rainy April and May. And the President helped us too. Two years ago we were getting a dollar a bushel, maybe a little less. But last year the government set the price at $2 a bushel—no more, no less. This year we'll clear almost $6,500! The Lord and the President be praised!

You will be surprised how much the children have grown. Jean Anne's too. Her place next door is doing fine. We're working together, Jean Anne and me, with some of our neighbors, working our farms like a team. It's not a new idea. But we're doing it year round. David said we should do it. I guess that's what he's learning in school.

We're sorry about why you're coming back but we'll be happy to see you again.
Your brother,
Duncan

Katherine looked out across the shimmering plain at the horizon.
Too far for me to see clearly, she thought, *much too far.*

Just before it pulled into Haywood, the train passed five rectangular wooden towers, forty feet high, built shoulder to shoulder along the tracks. Grain elevators—"prairie skyscrapers"—temporary storage for wheat that was shipped to the mills by rail.

When Katherine stepped down onto the platform, she saw Duncan standing there waiting for her, his son Daniel beside him, both looking as tall and solid as those towers.

Katherine carried two suitcases. The conductor, groaning and grimacing, managed to move her trunk onto the platform. She gave him a dollar and a smile. With a tip of his cap, he returned the smile.

Duncan leaned down to kiss Katherine on the cheek.
"Welcome."

He touched her shoulder lightly and asked, "How are you doing?"

"I'm doing fine."

"We're very sorry..."

"Thank you."

"And you'll stay as long as you like?"

"Yes. I will. Thank you."

Daniel kissed her other cheek.

"Hello, Aunt Katherine."

Katherine turned to him. "You've grown three or four feet since I saw you last. You're almost as big as your Dad."

"I'm not finished yet," Daniel said.

"You must be...seventeen. Eighteen...?"

"Eighteen," he said emphatically, as if "seventeen" were an insult.

"Help me with the trunk, Danny," his father ordered.

Duncan took one of the suitcases from Katherine and motioned for Daniel to take the other. Then, grasping opposite handles of the trunk, they lifted it.

"Wagon's right over there," Duncan said, leading Katherine along the platform.

The weathered wooden buckboard had two bench seats, one behind the other. The two-horse team was tied up to a hitching post. After they loaded the luggage onto the buckboard, Daniel climbed up to the rear seat and Duncan helped Katherine onto the front bench. Then he untied the horses and sat down beside her.

Katherine hadn't been in Haywood for almost three years. As they rode along Main Street, she could see that the town had grown. Now there were sidewalks everywhere, although the streets themselves were still unpaved. There were new businesses, new stores, a new restaurant. And automobiles were competing with the horse-drawn traffic. A shiny black two-seater, snorting angrily, passed the buckboard at an intersection, almost crashing into it.

"Too fast," Duncan said.

"Lots of cars in Boston?" Daniel asked.

"Lots of horses, too," Katherine answered.

"You ride in the city?" Duncan asked.

"I don't own a horse, but I rented one."

Duncan smiled. "Rented a horse? Imagine that."

"There was a stable a few blocks from the school," Katherine said.

Israel Berman's Stable on Charles Street, she thought. *Jeremy and I used to go riding together. He was surprised at how well...*

"You don't need to rent horses here," Daniel said. "No, ma'am. Not at McKenzie's."

"I guess when it comes to horses, Haywood is way ahead of Boston," Katherine said.

"Yes, ma'am," Daniel agreed.

"We've made some changes at home," Duncan said. "Black flies won't be at you anymore."

"Screens on the windows," Daniel explained proudly.

"And I bought a new windmill last year—all steel—and a new pump," Duncan said. "You can take a bath anytime you like. As many as you want."

But you still have to heat the water on the stove, Katherine thought.

"I don't think I'll miss Boston at all," she said.

In a few minutes, the town had disappeared. They were out on the plain. The sun was a blazing torch in the blue-white sky. A strong, hot south wind was blowing. That hadn't changed.

It was as if she had travelled back in time.

Where was Boston? It was a fantasy, a painful mirage, a thousand miles away, a thousand years away.

Kansas was a painful reality. And Katherine was caught somewhere in between.

She began to feel like a child again, the frightened child she had once been.

That night, exhausted as she was, Katherine couldn't fall asleep.

Duncan had done his best. He had bought a new mattress for an old bed. He had moved a square wooden chest of drawers into the room and hung a mirror on the wall behind it.

The shadowy bulk of her mother's upright piano hugged the wall in the moonlight.

A sly, surprisingly soft wind kept whispering past the window into the emptiness surrounding her. She could hear that emptiness, feel the vastness of it.

In Boston, the walls were strong enough to shield her, to keep nature at bay. Not here. The house was a thin shell, too thin to protect her.

In farm country, everything—planting, growing, harvesting, calving, living, dying—moved in rhythm to the relentless cycles of nature, forces beyond your control. And there was no way to know what the next season would bring. Lean year or fat. Famine or feast.

Like most of his neighbors, Katherine's father had taken refuge in religion. It was an austere Methodist faith that encouraged good works but relied on God's grace, and frowned on alcohol, gambling and what her father called "finery": fashionable clothing, jewelry, cosmetics.

Earlier that evening at the dinner table, Duncan and his family had echoed Father's confident faith. They were simply dressed, plain spoken, and eager to do good works—to make Katherine feel at ease and at home.

Duncan's wife, Eleanor, asked, "Do you still enjoy teaching?"

She was a sturdy, graceful woman with a warm, comfortable smile.

"I do," Katherine said. "Of course, it's easy to teach the girls who want to learn."

"And the ones who *don't*?" Daniel wondered.

"I try to let the music teach them. If I find the right piece, the right melody, well... Sometimes that'll do it."

"Before we got married," Eleanor said, "I thought I might teach."

"You'd be a good teacher," Katherine said.

"Maybe so," Eleanor said. Then, shaking her head, "There's more than enough to keep me busy around here."

"There surely is," Katherine agreed.

"David's talked about teaching," Duncan said, with an obvious lack of enthusiasm.

David, a taller, thinner, more tentative version of his father, blushed and didn't respond.

"Is that so?" Katherine asked.

"Well..." David glanced at his father, who stared at his dinner plate, and then at his mother, who nodded permission.

"The Aggie College..." David began, "it's going to change things. *Every*thing."

"Everything?" That was Duncan.

David nodded. "New ways to farm. To do business. Better ways."

"That sounds exciting," Katherine said.

"Farming *is* a business," David said. "It should be run that way. Father agrees. Don't you?"

Reluctantly, Duncan nodded.

"Twenty years from now," David said, "there'll be more science in farming. More control."

"Only God controls the wind and the rain," Duncan said.

"Maybe someday, *we* will."

"That's prideful talk," Eleanor warned.

"Are you interested in teaching at the College?" Katherine asked, trying to calm the waters.

"Yes, Aunt Kathy," David said, very softly, watching Duncan.

"Barbara wants to teach," Emily said. She was a slender twelve-year-old, with a teasing smile. "That's why Davey wants to."

David blushed again.

"Who is Barbara?" Katherine asked.

"Davey's sweetheart," Emily said, laughing.

"Emily..." David began, but Duncan raised an index finger to stop him.

After a quiet pause, Katherine asked, "And what would *you* like to do when you grow up, Emily?"

Emily shrugged and said, "I don't know." She squinted, concentrating on the future. "Play the piano? Like you do."

"Really?"

"Could you teach me?"

Katherine remembered her lessons, separated by her mother from the other children, shielded from the harsh farm labor, alone in a world the others never shared with her.

"I could," Katherine said, "but it takes lots of practicing."

"How much?" Emily asked.

"To begin with, maybe an hour a day. Every day. For a long time."

"How long?"

"Years." She looked at Duncan. "And you'd be by yourself, mostly. All alone."

"Would you like to try, Emmy?" Eleanor asked.

Emily nodded.

Katherine had hoped to discourage her. On this first night with her family, the last thing she wanted to do was revisit her past.

"Can I, Mother?" Emily asked.

"Yes, you can."

The wind had picked up speed. Its voice was now a strong, steady stage whisper in a wordless language.

I never imagined it would be so easy to leave Boston behind me, Katherine thought.

It may have been the familiar house, the familiar faces, or even the familiar fears, but she was able to reanimate her childhood, with its raw pleasures and Spartan comforts—its kerosene lamps and outdoor privies—with a large family in the close quarters that somehow bred an enhanced sense of privacy.

Katherine was determined to reshape herself to match the way they lived. To wear no make-up—except lipstick (and a touch of perfume). Pull her hair back and tie it with a ribbon (a pretty one). Buy some plainer dresses (but not too plain) and denim trousers for riding. (She had $100 in cash with her, and a bank check for $845, her life savings, which she would deposit in the Wasape Valley Bank in Haywood.)

She wanted to fit in as well as she could.

And she wanted to change the look in her sister Jean Anne's eyes.

Jean Anne and her husband, Boyd Richmond, had come to visit with Katherine after dinner. Boyd was a quiet, pleasant man who owned a neighboring farm.

Jean Anne was four years younger than Duncan but, to Katherine, she had always seemed much older—as if her youth were really a disguise. When Katherine was a child, the look in Jean Anne's eyes—deep, gray, remote, neither condemning nor forgiving—had almost frightened her. That look hadn't changed. Although Jean Anne smiled and asked the right questions and said the right things, Katherine still felt that her sister was watching her from a distance, an icy mountaintop, like an eagle preparing to strike.

She was never unkind to me, Katherine thought, *but she was always far away on that mountaintop.*

Katherine turned over, restlessly, uneasily.

Her mother's upright piano floated in the moonlight, like a dark, clumsy ghost. Katherine hadn't touched it yet. She remembered its sound, duller and thinner than the grand pianos at the Conservatory and the Academy.

Father asked Mother to play for the church services, Katherine thought, *but she told him she never would.*

"I don't believe in God," she said, "My music belongs to me."

However, she did go to church on Sundays, sang the hymns and recited the prayers.

"I do it for your father," she told Katherine. "But it leaves a bitter taste in my mouth."

They still call this the "music room," Katherine thought and she smiled.

She closed her eyes and tried to remember Jeremy's face, the sound of his voice, the taste of his lips, the taut circle of his arms around her, but those memories were beginning to fade.

"We have lost him," Amos Greene had said.

And now, gradually, relentlessly, Katherine was losing him.

Her eyes filled with tears. A few minutes later she fell into a dreamless sleep.

IV.

Katherine awoke early, but the family had already completed the first morning chores. She washed at the sink in the bathroom, pumping cold water into the basin.

After careful consideration, she decided on a simple tan dress and tied back her hair with a bright yellow ribbon. She joined the family at the breakfast table.

Eleanor served her a platter of scrambled eggs and salt pork, a thick slice of bread and a cup of coffee. Katherine spread sweet-tart apple jelly onto the bread. The apples grew in a one-acre orchard to the east of the house.

"Did you sleep well?" Eleanor asked.

"Yes, thank you."

"Mattress all right?" Duncan asked.

"Very comfortable."

"No black flies," Daniel said, with a trace of smugness.

"Not one," Katherine agreed.

"Are you going to play the piano for me today?" Emily asked, impatiently.

Katherine nodded. "Later. This afternoon."

"Promise?"

"Emily, don't be rude," Eleanor advised.

"I promise," Katherine smiled. "But I'd like to go to town this morning. I want to open a bank account. And buy some things."

"I'm headed for Haywood," David said. "Picking up some books I ordered. You can come with me."

"That would be nice."

"If you go with Davey, you'll meet Barbara," Emily said, with a conspiratorial smile.

David blushed. "She ordered some books, too."

"I look forward to meeting her," Katherine said. "But I have a few chores to do. If you're only picking up some books..."

"We're going to the Bluebell Restaurant, too," David said. "Ice cream sundaes."

"I hope you're not spending *all* your money on that young lady," Eleanor said, but her tone was friendly, teasing.

"No, ma'am."

"If you're sure I won't be keeping you..." Katherine said.

"I'm sure."

"Barbara lives down by the river," Eleanor volunteered.

"Good land," Duncan said, "but her father had to borrow money. A sizeable loan. For new equipment. Major repairs. He's having trouble paying it back."

"He's not happy about the price of wheat," David said.

"Why not?" Katherine asked.

"He says there's so much demand now, it would be higher than two dollars. Maybe as high as three dollars. But the government won't allow it."

"Thank the Lord we don't owe much," Duncan declared. "Nothing we can't take care of. Paid off the combine two years back."

"God willing, we'll have a good harvest next year, too," Eleanor said.

"God willing, the war will be over by then," Duncan added, looking at David.

Eleanor whispered, "God willing."

While David hitched a team of horses to the buckboard, Katherine waited on the porch.

The McKenzie farm stretched out all around her, reminding her of the world she had left, the world she had returned to.

The dark-steel windmill, turning its face as the currents shifted, its vanes humming steadily in the wind.

The apple orchard, where the fruit ripened until picking time in the

Fall. Most of the apples were sold, though some became home-made jelly or preserves.

The garden—watered, like the orchard, by the windmill: tomatoes, carrots, potatoes and sweet potatoes, cabbage, spinach, squash, pumpkins, blueberries, strawberries.

The barn—milk cows and horses.

The fenced-in pasture.

The chicken coop and pig sty.

Behind the barn, a heavily-insulated ice house which replenished the ice box in the storm cellar.

And covering most of Duncan McKenzie's 220 acres, the wheat fields. Now, after the June harvest, the wheat stubble—what was left of the plants—had been ground up and mixed with the dirt, killing the weeds and aerating the soil so the rain could soak in.

In September, the new crop of winter wheat would be planted with a "drill," digging wide rows of deep furrows, dropping wheat seeds into them and covering them with a thin layer of soil.

The new wheat cycle would start. The plants sprouting, green when the winter began. Dormant in the cold weather. Coming to life and growing again in the spring. Producing seeds and pollinating them. Then, in the early summer, when the plant itself had already died, the wheat seeds, the kernels, would be harvested.

But there were always "ifs." *If* the wind blows too hard at harvest time, the wheat kernels may fall to the ground before they can be gathered. *If* it rains at harvest time, the farmer must wait until the plants dry out before he can separate the stalks from the kernels. And *if* the fields are too wet, the combine might not be able to move through the mud.

A self-sufficient world, Katherine thought, *almost. But you never can be sure. All the hard work can be washed away by the next big storm or the next bitter drought.*

David drove the buckboard up to the front of the house.

"We can go now," he said.

Katherine climbed onto the bench beside him. She had borrowed a straw hat from Eleanor to shade her eyes.

Emily came out onto the porch and, as the buckboard pulled away, shouted, "Don't forget! When you come back!"

Katherine waved to her. "See you then!"

David drove onto the dirt road and turned north toward the Wasape River.

"How does it feel? Being here again?" he asked.

"I'm not sure. I'm between things."

"I hope you feel at home."

"I do. You've all been very kind."

The road wound between a small farm on the right and a broader expanse of fields on the left.

David pointed left and said, "Val Munson's place."

"As I recall, he wasn't a very good neighbor."

"Never had much to do with us, or anyone in town."

"A mystery man?"

David shook his head. "No mystery about it. He keeps to himself. Looks out for himself."

"And his son...a musician, I believe."

David nodded. "Val's wife died giving birth to Brad. Munson sent him away to school. He came back but he also keeps to himself. Like they say, the apple don't fall far from the tree."

"I guess that's so."

"Munson's always adding acres. He bought Ezra Pike's farm a couple of years ago. Pike owed a lot. Couldn't keep going. That's what Munson's done the past ten–fifteen years. Bought *three* farms. Got the most acreage in the county. Most of it's here. Some a few miles away, near Hickock."

"I guess he's doing what you said: running his farm like a business."

David frowned. "He's the one lent the money to Pike. And others, too. It was hard for them to make ends meet. He knew that. Put pressure on them."

Katherine thought of Amos Greene.

"Some people would call him a 'good' businessman," she said.

"Not me."

"Or me."

"He has almost twenty-five hundred acres now. Doesn't do the work himself. Has five families renting from him. Some hired hands, too. And a 'manager' that tells 'em what to do."

It wasn't ten o'clock yet, but the temperature was rising rapidly, stoked by a pitiless July sun in a cloudless sky, abetted by a hot breeze.

It took about half an hour to reach Barbara's farm. She was sitting in the shade of the front porch. She came out to the buckboard.

Katherine climbed down.

"I'm Katherine, David's aunt."

"Nice to meet you," Barbara said and shook Katherine's hand energetically.

"Why don't you sit up front?" Katherine suggested.

"Thanks."

Barbara climbed up beside David and kissed his cheek.

"Mornin', Davey."

She was an intense young woman, who moved quickly, confidently. Her face was rather broad and strong-boned, but her bold blue eyes contrasted beautifully with her dark hair.

Katherine sat on the back bench.

As they continued on the road to Haywood, Barbara turned toward Katherine and asked, "Back home to stay?"

"No. I may be here for a few months. Maybe a little longer."

"Have you travelled a lot?"

"Not as much as I'd like," Katherine said. "Too busy studying. And teaching."

"I'd like to travel someday," Barbara said. "Somewhere with mountains and seashore." She sighed. "*Everywhere.*"

David laughed. "She means Paris, London, Rome."

"Why not?" Barbara asked.

"There's a war on, remember?" David said.

"It won't last forever."

"You're very young," Katherine said. "No reason you can't see the world. Someday."

Barbara nodded vigorously. "No reason at all."

David nodded, too, but without much enthusiasm.

She may outgrow him, Katherine thought. *She may want more than he can give her.*

As the road turned toward the southeast, toward Haywood, they rode along the narrow, winding Wasape River, past massive white oak trees and clumps of tall cottonwoods. Pink and purple prairie gentians, blue cornflowers and white morning glories lined the banks with bursts of summer color.

Despite the heat, her fears and her memories, Katherine allowed herself to enjoy the beauty of the moment.

Harry Mason, one of the managers of the Wasape Valley Bank in Haywood, looked up from Katherine's application and said, "Katherine McKenzie?" as if he didn't believe it.

He was a pudgy, sandy-haired man in his late twenties, with the tentative pride of someone who has recently been promoted.

"That is me, yes," Katherine said. She was seated across the desk from him. "I'm Duncan McKenzie's sister."

Mason leaned back in his chair and studied her face.

"You left Haywood a long time ago."

"Almost fifteen years."

"And you've come home at last."

Katherine shook her head. "Just for a visit."

Mason smiled. "I remember you, Miss McKenzie."

"Really?"

"I was a little older than you." He laughed. "Still am."

"I'm sorry, Mr. Mason, but I don't..."

"I thought you were, well, the prettiest girl I ever saw."

He leaned forward, tried to look down at Katherine's application, but glanced up at her again.

"I don't think you ever told me so," she said. "I wouldn't have forgotten that."

"No. I was much too shy," Mason said.

"Well, it's nice of you to tell me now."

He leaned back in his chair and became the bank manager again.

"Please don't misunderstand me, Miss McKenzie. I'm a married man. Happily married. *Quite* happily married."

"You were just—remembering."

Reassured, Mason echoed, "Just remembering. We weren't farmers. My father owned the general store."

"Of course. Mason's. We shopped there."

"He sold the place. Four years ago." He curled his lip. "Now the town has a *department* store, Schaefer's. Like you have back east."

"Well, *you're* in a business with a real future."

Mason nodded. "Very true, Miss McKenzie. I'm in the right place. At the right time."

"And you're the right person to open my bank account."

"Delighted to do it," Mason said, back on safe ground.

He filled in some lines on the application and reached into an open desk drawer for a new bankbook. He wrote Katherine's name and account number on the first page.

"Please give this passbook and your check to one of the tellers. That's all there is to it."

He stood up and Katherine did, too.

"As I recall," Mason said, "you went east to study music. The piano."

"I did."

"You know, a few of us musicians—amateurs, of course—get together now and then, on an evening. Usually in my home. I play the cello. There are two fiddle players and a pianist, my wife."

"That sounds very nice."

"We play Mozart. Haydn. Even Bach. As well as we can."

"That's wonderful."

Katherine smiled and started to walk away.

Mason came around the desk and intercepted her.

"Would you consider, one evening, joining us?" he asked.

"Perhaps, I might. One evening."

"Is that a promise?"

"A possibility," Katherine said and after a pause, "I've been thinking of teaching here."

"My daughter is seven years old," Mason said. "A good time to start?"

"A perfect time."

"I could spread the word among my friends. I'm sure they'd be interested."

"I would be grateful for that."

"And you'll play for us? With us?"

"I will," Katherine said.

Mason smiled, sealing the bargain.

Schaefer's Department Store on Main Street was a block-long, two-story brick building with large display windows on the first floor.

Katherine bought a straw hat, two pairs of denim pants and two shirts (she couldn't ride horseback in a skirt, and her jodhpurs were inappropriate), and two simple, belted cotton dresses—one robin's-egg blue, one lime green.

The sales clerk in the clothing department told her that Mrs. Grady in Bedding was also in charge of the Music Department.

Mrs. Grady, a red-faced, buxom woman in her late forties, was striding purposefully between the blankets and the mattresses when Katherine approached her.

"Mrs. Grady? I'd like to buy some staff paper," Katherine said.

"Yes, yes," Mrs. Grady responded. "This way, please."

Katherine followed her to a niche behind Bedding. The Music Department consisted of a modest display of instruments—two guitars, a five-string banjo and a trumpet—three or four instructional manuals, sheet music of popular songs, and a random selection of religious, classical and semi-classical piano pieces.

Mrs. Grady stationed herself behind the counter, opened a drawer and took out a package of staff paper.

"There you are, dear," she said. "Just passing through town?"

"No, I'll be here for a while. I'm Duncan McKenzie's sister, Katherine. Home for a visit."

Mrs. Grady's efficient eyes softened a bit. "The McKenzies. I see Eleanor in here now and then. You're a musician, aren't you? A pianist, is it?"

"Yes."

"The staff paper... A composer, too?"

"Just dabbling."

Mrs. Grady sighed. "There's not much music hereabouts. Outside of church, of course."

"I don't do any concertizing these days," Katherine said. "But I was hoping to take on a few pupils while I'm here. I'd appreciate it if you'd mention that to your customers."

"Pupils?" Mrs. Grady's face became a little redder. "Children, you mean?"

"Well, if any adults..."

"You know, I've always wanted to play. The piano. Miss Boone, the organist at the Methodist church, teaches. But she's so gloomy. I suppose it's too late."

Katherine smiled. "Not at all."

"You think I could...?"

"Why not?"

Mrs. Grady smiled, too. "Why not. I *have* a piano. My mother left it to me. She played. I've tried learning on my own, but..."

"We could meet at your house."

"That would be—I'd be so pleased, if you would."

"We could start as soon as you like."

Mrs. Grady's complexion cooled down. "You know, there's another musician in Haywood. A pianist. Studied in Chicago. And New York City."

"My brother wrote me about him. In one of his letters. Val Munson's son?"

"Yes. Bradley. He buys reams of staff paper. He has me order music for him all the time. But as far as I know, he never plays anywhere. Except at home." She lowered her voice and added, "He's a strange one."

Like me, perhaps? Katherine wondered. *Afraid of audiences?*

"He may not be a performer," Katherine said. "I haven't done much of that myself. I prefer teaching."

"He's twenty-three or -four, in perfect health, as far as I can tell. Spends time training horses. For racing. Came in first at last year's County Fair." She lowered her voice again. "But he wasn't drafted."

"He may have some medical condition that..."

"No, no, dear. The board has special exemptions for farmers. Essential to the war effort."

"Well, then..."

Mrs. Grady shook her head. "As if he ever did a lick of farming. The Munsons hire other people to do the work for them."

"So I've heard."

"When you've got Munson's money, you can get away with anything."

Katherine shrugged. "How much do I owe you?"

"Seventy-five cents, please."

"And shall we make a date for your first lesson?"

"Would Saturday morning be all right, dear?"

"Fine. Where do you live, Mrs. Grady?"

"Seventeen School Street. Three blocks north of Main. The house where I was born. I moved back ten years ago, when my husband died. No one there but me and my Aunt Bertie."

"Ten o'clock?"

"Yes."

"See you then."

Mrs. Grady reddened again. "How much will you be charging?"

Katherine hesitated.

Her mother had been her only teacher when she lived on the farm. She had no idea what a piano lesson should cost in a small Kansas town.

"Let's say—a dollar a lesson?"

Mrs. Grady nodded and said, "See you Saturday."

That afternoon, Katherine played her mother's piano for the first time in many years.

"I'd like to warm up. Practice for an hour or so," she told Emily. "Can you wait a little longer?"

Emily was not pleased. "An hour," she said, and she meant it.

Duncan was at a meeting of the local cooperative "business" he and five other farmers had formed. The meeting was at Boyd Richmond's place, so Jean Anne had come over to the McKenzie's to have lunch with Eleanor. She was a surprise addition to Katherine's audience.

I remember the way she watched me when I played, Katherine thought. *As if she were waiting for me to fail.*

Alone in the music room, Katherine stroked the worn keys of the past with a virtuoso's touch. The piano's voice was strong and husky but lacked some of the lyrical overtones that could give wing to flights of fancy.

Her fingers moved gracefully along the keyboard, coaxing the instrument to soften its voice, infusing some subtlety into its heavy tread.

At the end of an hour or so, she went into the kitchen. Eleanor and Jean Anne and Emily were seated at the table with Daniel.

Emily jumped up.

"Are you warm enough, Aunt Kathy?" she asked.

Katherine laughed. "I am. Please come in."

Emily sat on the bed. Daniel stood by the window. Eleanor and Jean Anne carried their chairs into the room and set them down close to the piano.

"This is Chopin's *Raindrop* Prelude," Katherine said.

She closed her eyes, shutting out the July heat and the murmur of the wind, shutting off the past and present, focusing on the spirit and structure of the piece until it surrounded her.

As she played, she managed to reshape the stolid tones of her mother's piano with delicacy and tenderness.

When she had finished, her audience applauded.

"Play more," Emily said. "Please!"

"That was beautiful," Eleanor said.

"It was, Aunt Kathy," Daniel said.

Jean Anne didn't say anything. She watched Katherine with her cool gray eyes.

She's still on that mountaintop, Katherine thought.

"Franz Liszt's *Leibestraum*," Katherine said.

Again, she immersed herself in the music. Again, her audience applauded and Emily asked her to play more.

"An Impromptu by Franz Schubert."

Applause.

"One more," Katherine said. "This is *Für Elise* by Beethoven. He must have composed this *For Elise*, but no one knows who Elise was or why he wrote it for her."

"A girl he loved?" Daniel asked.

He's old enough to have love on his mind.

"I like to think so," Katherine said.

She tried to imagine Beethoven the way Simon Levin had described him: "that poor devil shaping sound from silence, hearing his music only with his soul."

That poor devil in love?

She played with controlled passion and thought the familiar piece sounded newer, fresher.

When she had finished, she said, "That's all for now, if you don't mind."

"Thank you, Aunt Kathy," Daniel said.

"Thank you," Eleanor said.

"I want to play, too," Emily said.

"We'll start your lessons soon," Katherine promised.

"Tomorrow? After breakfast?"

"Tomorrow it is."

Emily smiled and ran out of the room.

Jean Anne remained after the others had left.

"I remember that melody," Jean Anne said.

"You do?"

Jean Anne was sitting with her hands clasped on her lap, her eyes searching some distant place in mid-air.

"I remember your mother playing it. And you playing it, too."

"So long ago," Katherine said.

"So long ago," Jean Anne repeated.

She stood up, smiled at Katherine and left the room.

V.

August 8, 1918

Dear Louise,

I hope all is well with you and Andrew and all our friends and colleagues. You must keep me up to date on everyone, including Simon, the King of Commonwealth Avenue.

It's odd to think that I left Boston only a few weeks ago. It seems much longer. I'm settled into a new routine on the fringes of my family. They have welcomed me in such a friendly way that I've begun to question my childhood feelings about them. The children—my nieces and nephews—can't believe that someone like me was born here. (I'm too pale, too thin, and I have a strange accent.) One of my sisters, Margaret, moved out to Nebraska when she got married. They rarely see her. They just don't have much time for visiting.

Their lives are built around the work they do. The harvest was over by the time I arrived and the new crop won't be planted until September. But they always have more to do. Growing fodder to feed the cattle and horses. Raising chickens and pigs. They have an apple orchard. There are cows to milk, eggs to gather, fruit and vegetables to pick, pigs to slaughter (!).

They're very frugal and optimistic and religious, which sometimes cheers me up and sometimes makes me feel worse.

This is hard to believe, but it took almost no time for me to forget electricity, telephones, indoor plumbing and paved roads. I've become a Kansas child again with a memory of another life in another world. I miss many things—I certainly miss <u>you</u>, Louise. (I don't miss the Greenes!) But I still don't know how or when—or <u>if</u>—I'll return to that world.

I have a new routine. I practice three hours a day on my mother's old upright. It has some character, but it doesn't compare to the instruments I'm accustomed to. Still, it serves me well. And for the past three days, I've even toyed with the Andante of my new Sonata. (I may include the clucking of a chorus of hens.)

I also have four students! All beginners. All struggling with Hanon's *exercises. (Thinking ahead, I brought a couple of copies of his first book.) One student is the lady who runs the Music section at the local department store, where there were <u>two</u> copies of Hannon. In Haywood, Kansas! Imagine that! I'm charging a dollar a lesson, and no one seems to mind. The department-store lady is in her forties and always dreamed of being a pianist. I suppose a dollar a week isn't a high price to pay for a dream.*

I'm also teaching my twelve-year-old niece, Emily, who is an eager pupil, but has virtually no talent. She tries. How she tries!

I have two other students—two children—seven and nine, and that requires a little explanation. When I opened a bank account in town, the manager remembered me. (I think he loved twelve-year-old me from afar!) He and his wife and two friends get together one evening a week for their own musicale. One of his friends—an elderly pharmacist—is actually quite proficient on the violin. I was invited to join them. It's pleasant to get together with such enthusiastic music lovers. And, in addition, I've gained two pupils—the daughter of the banker and the grandson of the pharmacist/violinist.

There is another pianist here, trained in Chicago and New York, living on a neighboring farm. His name is Bradley Munson. Local gossip has it that he never plays in public. (Does that sound familiar?) I hope to find out more about him: I'm going to try to see him this afternoon. (They say he's a recluse.) I may challenge him to Chopin at twenty paces.

I wish I could tell you that I'm closer to working things out, but I'm not. Please write and tell me all about the goings-on in my "other world."

Love,

Katherine

"You're wasting your time," Duncan said. "The Munsons don't mix with anyone else."

"I'd like to meet him," Katherine said.

Duncan shrugged.

They were eating lunch.

"I'm going to ride over," Katherine said.

She was wearing denim pants and a blue shirt.

Duncan smiled. "Then you and Matilda should get acquainted."

"Matilda?"

"Don't worry. She's friendly." He clicked his tongue a couple of times. "That'll get her going. Tap her barrel to speed her up."

"'*Ho*' to stop her," Daniel said.

"Not too complicated," Katherine observed.

"I'll saddle her up for you, Aunt Kathy," Daniel said.

"*I* can do that," Katherine said, smiling. "I was riding before you were born."

"Mind if I watch?" Daniel asked.

"Me, too?" That was Emily.

"I don't mind."

Matilda was a seven-year-old reddish-brown mare.

Katherine approached her slowly, repeating "Matilda, good girl," softly.

Matilda studied Katherine alertly but calmly, wondering who this newcomer was.

Still murmuring "Matilda, good girl," Katherine stroked the horse's neck, then her muzzle.

The mare lowered her head and turned toward Katherine—a signal that Matilda welcomed the caresses.

Now that they were acquainted, Katherine moved confidently, brushing the horse's coat from the withers across her back, putting on the saddle pad, then the saddle.

"Here we go, girl," Katherine said, tightening the cinches.

She glanced at Daniel and Emily, who nodded their approval.

She added the bridle and bit, and stroked Matilda's muzzle one more time.

"Good girl." She turned to Daniel and Emily. "Did I pass the test?"

They both nodded.

"Then Matilda and I are leaving."

She tipped her straw hat forward, mounted the horse, took the reins firmly in hand, clicked her tongue and rode out of the barn.

Katherine walked Matilda out to the road, with Daniel and Emily following a few steps behind. When they reached the road, Katherine tapped Matilda's flanks with her stirrups and the mare broke into a trot. Katherine turned in the saddle and waved to Daniel and Emily.

The day was warm, but not as hot as it had been for the past week. The south wind was so strong that Katherine pushed her straw hat down so it clung more tightly to her head.

There was a dark cloud showing the tip of its head over the southern horizon.

It's riding the wind, she thought. *No way to tell how soon it will reach us.*

She felt uneasy, but she didn't give in to the feeling. She tapped Matilda's barrel again and the horse began to canter. The mare had a long, easy stride. Katherine fell into the same rhythm, posting to match the horse's movements.

She felt her heart beating faster, echoing the mare's hoofbeats. She tapped Matilda's flanks again and the horse broke into a full gallop.

Cooler air rushed past Katherine's face. She felt a surge of excitement, as if she were suddenly weightless, a soft, white cloud—*not* a storm cloud—soaring in an endless blue sky. She breathed in the cool air, drank it down, as if it were a chilled white wine.

For the first time in a long time—the first time in years—she was alone with herself, living moment to moment, neither judging nor being judged, afraid only that the feeling would pass too soon.

When Katherine reached the side road that would take her onto Val Munson's farm—when she signaled Matilda to slow to a walk—the feeling did pass. But traces of it lingered, and she sensed that something within her was beginning to change.

Val Munson's place was a compact, two-story, white clapboard house, a surprisingly modest home for one of the wealthiest men in the county.

Katherine tied Matilda to the hitching post and walked up three steps onto the front porch. She knocked once, left a polite pause, and knocked a second time.

A tall, lanky man in his mid-thirties opened the door and stepped onto the porch quickly, as if he were guarding the entrance. His coarse brown hair was streaked with gray. His face was a leathery tan. He smiled at Katherine, but his dark eyes seemed less than friendly.

"Can I help you, ma'am?"

"I hope so. I'm Katherine McKenzie. My brother's farm is down the road."

"Max Caldwell," the man said. "I'm Mr. Munson's foreman."

Katherine extended her hand. Caldwell hesitated for a moment, then reached out and clasped it.

"Nice to meet you," she said.

Caldwell nodded. "Mr. Munson ain't here. He's in St. Louis. On business."

"Is Bradley with him?"

Caldwell shook his head.

"I'd like to meet him," Katherine said, adding, "Bradley."

"Meet him," Caldwell repeated thoughtfully, as if he had never heard those words before.

"Is he here?"

"Yes, ma'am."

"Then...?"

Caldwell began to speak, stopped, then said, "He ain't at the house."

"Do you expect him back soon, or...?"

"He's on the farm." He pointed to his left. "At his place. Down the road."

"He doesn't live here?"

Caldwell pursed his lips. "He does. He's got a—he calls it a 'studio'—down that road a piece."

"Would he mind if I called on him there?"

"I don't know, ma'am."

"Down that road, you said?"

"Not far. Past the orchard. Don't need your horse."

Katherine stepped back and smiled.

"Thank you, Mr. Caldwell."

"He don't like company, ma'am."

"Well, I can always turn around and go home."

Caldwell nodded.

Katherine left him standing stiffly at the door, a sentry at his post.

After a ten-minute walk, Katherine turned the corner of the apple orchard. Now she could see Bradley's "studio," a small white clapboard replica of the main house. And she began to hear a flood of piano music. It was a breathless torrent of sound, notes piled on notes, surging from dissonance to consonance and back again.

Katherine stood near the door listening, trying to make sense of what she was hearing. Several different themes, in different keys and disparate tempos, confronted each other in a seemingly chaotic, complex, illogical structure. After a minute or two, she thought she could identify one of the melodies, a Methodist hymn—"O Come and Dwell in Me"—played very slowly. Then she was almost certain she heard Stephen Foster's "Beautiful Dreamer" rushing by at high speed. And was that the wartime hit "Over There" lurking in the background, distorted but still recognizable?

Katherine was no stranger to music that stretched the traditional boundaries almost beyond their limits—Mahler, Schoenberg, Stravinsky. Younger composers, some of whom she knew, were trying to venture even further.

But no one has gone this far, she thought.

She raised her hand to knock on the door, but hesitated. The music seemed undisciplined, almost hysterical, and it had unnerved her.

A loud, dissonant chord abruptly staunched the torrent of notes.

Katherine waited. The silence eased the tension. She knocked on the door.

A long minute passed, then another, but she didn't dare knock again.

The door was opened by a lean young man in faded tan trousers and a checked shirt.

"Are you lost?" he asked.

"Not if you're Bradley Munson," Katherine said, smiling.

He didn't return the smile. "Who are *you*?"

"Katherine McKenzie. Duncan's sister."

"And...?"

"I wanted to meet you."

"And...?"

His eyes were a cold shade of blue, a wall of ice.

"I'm visiting my brother for a few months," Katherine said softly, "and I—"

Bradley sighed. "I'm busy."

He began to close the door.

"I'm a musician, too," Katherine said quickly.

"Uh-huh..."

"I heard you playing."

He opened the door again.

"I've never heard anything like it," she added.

"That's for sure."

"I'm sorry to disturb you if—"

"You're a musician?"

"Yes. A pianist. I studied at the New England Conservatory."

"That doesn't matter."

"I just thought—"

"When you study, you learn the rules. But rules don't matter."

"They do."

He ran his fingers through his thick blonde hair.

"*Breaking* them matters," he said.

Katherine didn't want to argue, but she didn't back down. "Don't you have to *know* them *before* you break them?"

He leaned against the door jamb and studied her more closely.

"You sound like a critic," he said, with a trace of a smile.

"Never."

"You live in Boston?"

"Yes."

"You play there?"

"I don't concertize."

"You don't."

"I teach."

"At the Conservatory?"

"At a school for young women."

He looked down at her hands. "A waste of time."

"I enjoy teaching."

Bradley frowned. "I doubt it."

"I've heard *you* don't perform in public, either."

"I did. Briefly. In Chicago. Very good reviews."

He paused.

Katherine smiled and said, "And...?"

Reluctantly, he smiled, too. "I wasted too much energy trying to be Chopin or Mozart."

He gestured for her to enter the studio.

It was a single large room with a row of four tall windows facing south toward the fields. There was a grand piano under the windows, a cot in one corner and, in the center, a table and two chairs.

"I learned to play so I could compose," he said.

"What I heard...?"

He nodded. "Would you like some wine?"

"Yes, thank you."

"I'm afraid all I have is Merlot."

"That will be fine."

He led her to the table and motioned for her to sit. From a cabinet against the wall, he brought back a bottle and two glasses. He sat down across from Katherine, filled the glasses and toasted, "The rules."

"The rules," she said.

The wine was mellow and pleasant.

"On vacation?" Bradley wondered.

"You could say that."

"What would *you* say?"

"I'm taking a break."

"School's out for the summer?"

"Yes."

"And you came all the way out to Kansas?"

"I grew up here."

"Family ties," he said.

"That's right."

"I *didn't* grow up here."

"I've heard you went away to school."

"I was *sent* away."

"Your father wanted you to see more of the world."

Bradley laughed contemptuously. "My mother died birthing me. I don't know what she was like. But he sure as hell wasn't made to be a father."

"It may seem that way..."

Bradley shook his head. "Please. I know him. You don't."

"I didn't mean to—"

"You came back to visit your family?"

"Not just that."

"To escape the police?"

Katherine laughed. "No. But I needed to get away."

"Let me guess. You broke up with your boyfriend."

"He... That's right."

"You'll find another one."

"That's what they tell me."

"How long have you lived in Boston?"

"I was twelve when I left the farm."

"Did you miss Kansas?"

"No. I never felt at home here. Still don't."

Bradley looked out the window at the fields. "This is a special place for me," he mused. "In Chicago, in New York, I missed Kansas."

"I didn't."

"How could you not?"

Katherine followed his gaze out the window. "It's too big. Too flat."

He waved his arms above his head. "I'd call it 'spacious.'"

"Too cold in winter. Too hot in summer."

"Challenging," Bradley said. "And there's a hell of a history. Bleeding Kansas. The Civil War. A battleground over slavery. John Brown. Quantrill's Raiders."

"I'm sorry I missed all that," Katherine said.

Bradley was undeterred. "After the war, Abilene and Dodge City. The end of the cattle drives. All the great gunslingers. Wild Bill Hickock. Wyatt Earp."

"My kind of people," she winked.

"Doesn't music have charms to soothe the savage breast?"

"But not the storms. The tornadoes."

Bradley sipped his wine and concluded, "That's the beauty of it. You can hear God singing. And shouting. And I love to shout back."

"God doesn't sing to me."

"Not a believer?" he wondered.

"I never was."

"When I lived in Chicago, I didn't think about God."

"Why not?" Katherine asked.

"I was too busy. But here..."

He shrugged.

Katherine heard the wind rushing past the windows.

"That doesn't sound like singing to me," she said.

"You're not listening."

"I am."

"Not with *my* ears."

"But I *did* hear you playing," Katherine said.

"Me, shouting back."

"Quite a shout."

"It's taking shape."

"It was—I'm not sure what it was."

"I think that means you didn't like it," Bradley said.

"I'd have to hear it again."

He didn't respond.

"More than once," she said.

"I'm breaking the rules."

"All of them, I think."

"Does that make you uncomfortable?"

"I don't mind being uncomfortable."

He pointed his finger at Katherine. "Then there's hope for you."

"Will you play for me?"

"Not now."

"Next time?"

"I haven't invited you back."

The wine had made Katherine a little braver.

"You didn't invite me today, either."

"True. I guess I can't stop you from barging in."

"You can't."

She pointed to her empty glass. He refilled it.

"Tell me about the piece you were playing."

Slowly sipping his wine, Bradley shifted his gaze out the window again, then studied Katherine's face for a minute or two.

"I'm working it out on the piano. I'll orchestrate it later."

He paused, leaned forward and said, "It's a mixed bag—everything that's going on. And everyone who's doing it. In a small town and the farms around it. My town. (I may call it that.) Not broken into pieces, but all together. Hymns and dance music. Popular songs. Country fiddles. And at the same time, the sounds of the farmhouses and streets. The combines and drills. The horses and cattle. Different keys, different tempos. Different moods. Clashing, harmonizing and clashing again."

He leaned back and added, "I've been at it for almost a year."

"Have you played it for anyone yet?"

"No. My father built this place so I wouldn't bother him."

"He's not interested in your work?"

"Money. Women. That's what he's about."

Bradley stood up.

"Maybe no one will ever hear it."

"Except me?"

"We'll see," he said.

Katherine took a last long sip of wine.

"I'm glad I met you," she said, rising.

Bradley didn't answer her.

He opened the door with a silent nod.

"Keep listening," he said as she left.

Walking toward the main house, Katherine glanced at the southern horizon. The storm clouds were much closer and the wind was kicking up.

She moved more quickly, almost running to reach Matilda. The mare was placidly munching on a few strands of grass near the hitching post. Katherine untied her, mounted and in a few minutes was galloping down the road toward the McKenzie farm.

A crackle of lightning flashed close by, followed a few seconds later by a growl of thunder.

Is God singing? she thought. *Or is He just shouting at me?*

The storm was darkening the skies, racing toward her on legs of lightning. The road into the McKenzie farm was still a quarter mile away. A moment later she felt the first wind-driven spray of rain, wrapping its wet arms around her and clouding her vision.

The mellowness of the wine had faded. She was afraid.

She reached her brother's farm at a gallop and didn't slow to a walk until she was a few yards from the barn. She dismounted, led Matilda into the barn, took off the saddle and bridle and put the mare back in her stall.

Katherine ran to the house. She was wet to the skin.

"Did you meet him?" Eleanor asked.

"I did. We talked."

"About music."

"Yes."

Lightning flashed and thunder followed almost immediately.

"Thank the Lord. We can use the rain," Eleanor said.

"I have to get out of these clothes."

"Would you like a cup of tea?"

"Yes. Thank you."

As she removed her wet clothing, Katherine listened to the sounds of the storm, the angry voice of the wind, the slashing rhythm of the rain against the roof and the windows.

She tried to listen with Bradley's ears, but she couldn't.

VI.

August 12, 1918

Dear Katherine,

I enjoyed your letter. It was almost as good as talking to you face to face. Almost, but not really.

It has been a very bad summer. Father works late almost every day and when he's home he spends a lot of time in the den. Mother sleeps late and usually has her meals in her bedroom. She goes to church on Sundays and sometimes during the week, which she never did before, but she doesn't go out otherwise. And she never has dinner parties anymore. I eat alone most of the time. We miss Jeremy so much.

The war keeps going on. Is anyone winning? It's the soldiers who are losing. In one story I read, a general was talking about how machine guns and poison gas were making the "butcher's bill" bigger and bigger. The butcher's bill! That's what he called the men who are dying. Well, he's in no danger!

And now we have another war in Boston. There's been an outbreak of influenza among the dockworkers that has spread to the sailors who live in the barracks by the water. People are getting sick in other parts of town, too. It's really dangerous. They get high fever with terrible coughing and it's killed some people. It's spreading. There's no cure.

Father tells me I have to stay home, away from my friends so I won't catch it. But I go out sometimes anyway. He says there's a shortage of doctors because so many of them went into the army.

Some people say there were Germans who came ashore from a U-Boat and spread the influenza germs in the water.

I'm sorry to be so gloomy, Katherine. But I want to tell you the truth the way I always did. I want to be your friend. Always.

Love,

Jamie

Katherine's second visit to Bradley's studio was on a warm, muggy Monday morning, a week after their first meeting. He wasn't there. When she walked back to the house, Max Caldwell was sitting on the steps.

"Miss McKenzie," he said.

"Mr. Caldwell, how are you today?"

"Fine, ma'am. Yourself?"

"I'm well, thank you. I was just at the studio. Bradley isn't there."

"No, ma'am. He's at the track."

"The track?"

"Brad has a horse he's trainin'."

"I've heard he's won some races."

"One or two."

"So he's at the racetrack today?"

"No, ma'am. There's a practice track on the farm. That's where he's at."

"Could you tell me how to get there?"

Caldwell pointed to a road that ran northwest, at a sharp angle to the house.

"It's more 'n a mile from here. You might want to ride."

"Thank you, Mr. Caldwell."

"Yes, ma'am."

As Matilda cantered down the road, Katherine looked out at Val Munson's broad acres of dark farmland, ready for planting. She knew that the McKenzies would be "drilling" soon—the first week of September.

About a half mile from the Munson house, she saw a trim, one-story white cottage not far off the road. A woman in bib overalls was working in the vegetable garden near the cottage.

Renters, Katherine thought. *Making Val Munson richer. Not much left for themselves.*

She tried not to think about that.

She tapped Matilda's flanks and the mare began to gallop. The warm air became a little cooler and Katherine felt lighter, freer, less earthbound.

If I knew where I was going, she thought, *where I should be going... I wouldn't stop until I got there.*

But she still didn't know.

The practice track was a dirt path thirty feet wide and a quarter-mile in circumference, cut through a grassy meadow. A wire fence surrounded it.

Katherine rode along the fence for a few yards until she came to a gate. She dismounted and tied Matilda's reins to the fence. The mare began to sample the local grass.

Katherine could see Bradley on the opposite side of the track in a sulky—a light, two-wheeled cart—pulled at high speed by a squarely-built chestnut horse. As they approached her, Katherine waved at Bradley, but he didn't seem to notice.

The horse's flanks were glossy with sweat, its nostrils flaring, its dark eyes searching for an imagined finish line.

As they passed her, Bradley slapped the shaft of the sulky with a long, light whip and the horse—a stallion—responded to the signal by picking up speed.

Katherine remembered the excitement of harness racing at county fairs when she was a child. The posters advertising the fairs usually featured the races as the main attraction.

Sometimes the horses were trotters. They ran with an awkward stride—right foreleg and left hindleg moving forward and back together, and then the opposite pair doing the same. Even the best trotters often broke stride, losing the race—and the money of those who bet on them.

Pacers were more popular. They were a little faster than trotters and they rarely broke what seemed like a more natural stride—forelegs and hindlegs on the same side, moving forward and back together.

Bradley's stallion was a strong, spirited pacer.

He drove around the track and passed Katherine again. This time Bradley noticed her, but he raced for one more lap before he slowed down and cooled off the horse with a much slower final lap.

He stopped by the gate where she was standing.

"Morning," he said.

"I hope you didn't mind me watching."

"Not at all."

Bradley got off the sulky, led the horse to the gate and opened it.

"His name's Legato," he said.

"Charming."

"Because he runs so smoothly," Bradley added.

"He's beautiful," she said admiringly.

Bradley nodded. "Good bloodlines."

He led Legato through the gate, then closed it. He climbed back onto the sulky.

"The barn's near the main house. Ride along with me."

She mounted Matilda and matched the mare's pace to Legato's.

"I was hoping to hear you play today," Katherine said.

"Not today."

Katherine let the silence speak for her.

After a minute or two, Bradley said, "I just don't feel—I'm tired."

"I understand."

"I'm in a racing mood."

"I can see that."

"You're disappointed."

"I am."

After a long pause, Bradley said, "We should get to know each other better."

"I'd like that."

"After a workout, I often go down to the river with a picnic basket. Wine and cheese. Come with me."

"Will you bring your piano?" Katherine asked.

"No, but maybe I can cheer you up anyway."

"You already have."

In the barn, Bradley cooled off the stallion, sponging him down with a couple of pails of water. He brushed Legato's coat briskly and fed him some hay.

"They say a horse shouldn't drink right after a workout," Bradley said. "They're wrong."

"Breaking the rules again?"

He smiled. "A horse drinks just what he needs. *Mine* does, anyway."

He filled Legato's trough with water.

"After I saddle up Lucifer, we'll get the vittles at the house." Bradley said.

"Lucifer?"

"He's not the Devil at all. Just the opposite. A kind old beast."

A few minutes later, they walked their horses over to the house. Max Caldwell was no longer on guard.

Bradley tied Lucifer to the hitching post and started up the steps. He turned and motioned to Katherine.

"I can wait here," she said.

"Come with me."

Katherine slipped Matilda's reins over the hitching post and followed Bradley up the steps and into a central hallway. There was a large study on the left, the walls lined with half-empty bookshelves. On the right was a simply-furnished dining room. Bradley led Katherine through the dining room into the kitchen.

"The cook's off duty," he said. "Good time to steal some food."

He took a picnic basket from a shelf over the range, three or four cloth napkins from another shelf, two wine glasses, and a knife from a rack on the counter. He foraged in the ice box and found a wedge of brie and an unopened bottle of white wine.

"I made sure the wine would be chilled," he said.

"Good planning," Katherine said.

"Ah! Strawberries! The cook's going to be mad at me for taking them."

He carefully put the vittles into the picnic basket and secured the lid.

Katherine followed him back through the dining room.

"Mornin', Brad."

Val Munson was standing in the doorway of the study. He was a short, barrel-chested man with long, gray-blond hair and a full, gray beard.

"Mornin', Pa."

Munson studied Katherine for a moment, from head to toe and back again.

"Max said you was takin' up with a girl."

"Good old Max," Bradley said.

Munson smiled unpleasantly. "'Bout time."

"This is Katherine McKenzie," Bradley said. "Duncan's sister."

"Pleased to meet you," Munson said.

"My pleasure," Katherine said, although it wasn't.

"He play the piano for you?" Munson asked.

"I've—heard him play."

"Makes a hell of a lot o' noise, don't he?"

"I—"

Munson smiled again. "Had to get him out o' the house. Couldn't stand the noise."

"Well, I think he—"

"Wasted a lot o' my money so they could teach him to make all that noise."

Bradley, ignoring his father, opened the front door.

"We're going, Pa," he said.

"Don't worry, Miss, you're safe with Brad," Munson said.

"I'm not worried."

"Safer than you'd be with me, that's for sure," Munson added.

"For sure," Bradley said.

Bradley's favorite spot was on the bank of the Wasape River in the shade of a massive white oak tree. They sat on a flat-topped boulder that served as a picnic table.

They drank Chardonnay, ate cheese and strawberries, and listened to the soft music of the riverwater.

"Nothing like this in Boston," Bradley said.

"That's true."

"Or New York. Or Chicago."

She nodded. The wine, the shade, the riverflow soothed her.

"You love working with that horse, don't you?" Katherine said.

"He and I understand each other."

"I've heard you're a winner."

Bradley drank some wine, ate a strawberry and said, "One big race last year. At the Haywood Fair. Against some professionals. Just luck."

"Are you racing again in September?"

"Yes. I don't have a great horse. He's good, but he's no Dan Patch. And I'm not a great driver. Probably won't win."

He paused, as if he were deciding whether to confide in her.

"It's the feeling I get," he said, "even when we're just working out."

"What feeling?"

"Like there's nothing else in the world but us."

"Freedom," Katherine said.

"Freedom."

"I've felt that, too, sometimes."

Bradley looked out at the sunlit plains and said, "Out here?"

"Yes."

"Not in Boston."

Katherine smiled. "Not that I recall."

"The Kansas girl in you."

Katherine wondered if that were true.

"I went to church yesterday," Katherine said.

"And you found God? In the next pew."

"I felt the way my mother did, years ago. I didn't belong there."

"Nothing wrong with that," Bradley said.

"Feeling alone?"

"You don't belong to other people."

"I don't want to be alone."

Bradley drank some wine, reflected for a moment and said, "In Chicago, I was engaged. To a painter. Very talented."

"A composer. A painter. *La Boheme.*"

"She couldn't carry a tune."

"But it *was* romantic."

"That was the problem."

"Why?"

"It doesn't last."

"How do you know—?"

"I broke the engagement."

"That's sad."

"Marriage would have been sadder."

Bradley refilled their wine glasses.

"Why did *your* romance become unromantic?" he wondered.

"It didn't."

"You said—"

"*I* was engaged, too," Katherine said. "Jeremy is his name. He was in the army. In France. He was killed."

"A widow. Never a wife," Bradley said.

"I came here—I need—I'm not sure..."

"And you're willing to talk to me—the notorious draft dodger?"

"Jeremy volunteered."

"A hero!" Bradley said, frowning.

"I didn't want him to."

"Uncle Sam needed him."

"He was scared."

Bradley nodded and said, "So am I. I have things I want to do. Dying isn't one of them."

He added, "They hate me around here. I'm Val Munson's son. That's bad enough. I won't be marching off with *their* sons. That's worse."

"I don't hate you."

"I was supposed to be cheering you up," he said. "I'm not doing a very good job."

"You could play for me," Katherine said, smiling.

"I will. Not today."

Katherine listened to the waterflow and sipped her wine.

"This is a beautiful spot," she said.

"I'm usually here alone," Bradley said.

"I'm not spoiling it for you?"

"No," he said.

"You don't mind being alone," Katherine said.

"I don't."

"You didn't enjoy performing? Hearing applause?"

"No."

"Don't you want people to listen to your music?"

Bradley shrugged.

"I'm sure they'd hate it." He laughed. "But it'll never come to that. What orchestra's going to play a crazy piece of music by an unknown composer?"

"There are musicians—I know some—who might..."

"Finish the strawberries," Bradley said, holding out the bowl.

As Katherine ate the last two strawberries, Bradley asked, "Why don't *you* concertize?"

"I do care about audiences."

"Then you should be out there."

"I can play for colleagues. Friends," Katherine said. "But with strangers, audiences, I freeze."

"You've got to keep trying."

"When I was twenty. Twenty-three. Even as part of an ensemble, I can't."

"So you teach."

"When I was at the Conservatory..."

"Everyone was a competitor," Bradley said.

"Everyone planning *remarkable* careers!"

"Except you."

"Except me," Katherine agreed. "I was twelve when I arrived. An outsider. From Kansas! And that didn't change." Katherine's face reddened. "As time went by—I didn't live the life they did. Most of them."

"One lover after another."

"I didn't want to."

"You really *were* an oddity," Bradley said.

"My mother warned me."

"What mother doesn't?"

"But I took it to heart."

"You were careful. Nothing wrong with that."

"I was afraid."

"Of men like me."

Katherine nodded and smiled. "I guess Mother was right."

"What do you remember about her?" Bradley asked.

"She wasn't strong enough. For life out here. No Kansas girl in her."

"But you're a hybrid," Bradley said.

"I am."

"At least you remember her."

"Does your father talk about your mother?" Katherine asked.

Bradley's eyes grew cold. "Not much. A couple of years ago..."

He left the sentence in mid-air.

"A couple of years ago..." echoed Katherine, softly.

Bradley looked at her, remembering. "He was drunk. That's not unusual. I was drinking with him. That's *very* unusual."

He listened to the sound of the river as if it were reminding him of the past.

"He said Mother was beautiful. But a 'china doll.' Too weak. Like your mother, in a way."

"Like mine."

Bradley's voice saddened. "He said giving birth to me killed her."

"That's not fair."

"It's true."

"Not the way he meant it," Katherine said.

"He cared about her. I can't picture that."

Bradley poured the last half-inch of wine into Katherine's empty glass.

"Here's to cheering you up," Bradley said.

Katherine said, "Next time."

VII.

She was running toward a farmhouse as fast as she could, but she could never reach it in time. Behind her, gaining on her, the tornado roared—a twisting, savage whirlpool of wind—devouring wheat fields and orchards and barns, unstoppable, omnipotent, a mindless, angry god, a second or two away from swallowing her.

Suddenly, the fierce wind died. The farmhouse disappeared. She was running across a barren, cratered field. Flashes of light and bursts of sound exploded around her. She could hear hundreds—thousands of voices crying out in pain. She was approaching someone—a soldier on his knees, wounded, bleeding. He looked up at her. Jeremy. She tried to call out his name but she was mute. She stopped in front of him, reached out her hand and brushed the blood from his face. It wasn't Jeremy. It was Bradley. He shouted, "Listen!" She tried to scream but she couldn't.

She woke up shivering, breathing hard. As she lay in the darkness, pushing away the nightmare, she felt something more disturbing than fear. Guilt. Bradley was coming between her and Jeremy, even in her dreams.

At dinner that evening, she hadn't spoken about her riverside picnic with Bradley. But his name had come up.

Duncan and Eleanor were quieter than usual at the dinner table.

Emily was unhappy.

"Aunt Kathy, my fingers are too stupid to learn. Too stupid!"

"Don't be discouraged," Katherine said. "It takes time."

"I'm trying hard."

"I know you are."

"*Very* hard."

"Just keep practicing."

"I'll never play as good as you," Emily said.

"It's too soon to tell."

Emily was unconvinced. She looked down at her hands and stage-whispered, "Stupid!"

"You can do it," Daniel said.

"You can, sweetheart," Eleanor said, but she seemed distracted.

"David registered for the draft today," Duncan said.

Katherine could feel the tension rise.

"Anyone who'll be twenty-one this year had to," David said. "That's me. In November."

"Doesn't mean you'll be drafted," Duncan observed.

"I'm Class One," David said. "Nothing to stop them from taking me."

"You can appeal," Eleanor said. "You're doing farm work. That's 'essential,' isn't it?"

"Only if your name is Munson," David said.

Everyone looked at Katherine.

"Aunt Katherine lost someone," Duncan said. "She understands."

"Yes, I do," Katherine said.

"Then why do you—?" David began.

"David, please..." Eleanor interrupted him, but Katherine could see the same question in her eyes.

"I know. It's not fair," Katherine said.

"Fighting wars. Why?" Eleanor asked. "In places we never heard of."

"We'll appeal," Duncan said.

"Harry Mason wasn't drafted," Katherine said. "I could ask him..."

Eleanor shook her head. "He had a terrible fever one summer. He was three or four. Damaged his heart."

There was little conversation after that. When dinner was over, Katherine went out for a walk.

Duncan followed and caught up with her.

"Seem like we're ganging up on you?" he asked.

"I don't blame you."

"I don't blame Val Munson. I'd do anything for my boys, too."

They were walking along the border of the apple orchard. The spinning, humming steel vanes of the windmill were a shadowy blur in the moonlight.

"You and Bradley...?" Duncan let the sentence trail off.

"We're just—talking."

"Can't say we really know him. Left when he was a youngster. Came back, now and then. But not for long."

"His father seems very—unpleasant."

Duncan smiled. "Years ago, Val and I were friends. Not close, but friends. He's a little older than me."

"Friends? With him?"

"Even back then, he was always thinkin' about money. But not in a mean way."

"Did you know his wife?"

Duncan nodded. "Sweet little girl. Shy. Very young when she married him. She sang in the church choir."

"It's hard to imagine him with a wife like that."

"When she died... We never saw him in church after that."

"I know how he feels."

"I could see that," Duncan said, "on Sunday."

Katherine stopped and turned to him.

"I'm sorry if—"

"Nothin' to be sorry about. Your mother. She was with us every Sunday. But she didn't want to be."

"If I don't come with you, your neighbors will—"

"Don't worry about that."

"But—"

"Katherine, I try to believe. But you can't look around and not wonder."

"Would *you* create this kind of world?" Katherine asked.

"Don't think so."

"It doesn't make any sense."

"Doesn't seem to," Duncan said.

He smiled. "Maybe the next world..."

"Maybe."

Duncan looked up at the moon. "*That's* kinda pretty. Don't think I could do better."

"No one lives there. If we did, it wouldn't be so pretty."

Duncan laughed. "Apple pie for dessert. Eleanor made vanilla ice cream! Want some?"

"I do," Katherine said.

They walked back to the house.

When Bradley opened the door of the studio, his eyes brightened. "Lots of clouds this morning, Kathy. A storm coming. Surprised you're here."

"Don't disappoint me," Katherine said.

At the picnic a week earlier, Bradley had promised to play his music for her "next Wednesday—no, let's make it Thursday. At ten in the morning."

"Would you like some coffee?" he asked.

There was a small wood-burning stove in a corner of the room. A coffeepot sat on top of it.

"I had breakfast, thank you," Katherine said, not hiding her impatience.

Bradley walked toward the piano, but when he reached it he stopped and turned around.

"Would you do me a favor?" he asked.

"A favor?"

"Play for me."

Katherine sighed and said, "It's *your* music I came to hear."

"You will."

"I'm beginning to wonder."

"Professional courtesy," Bradley said, but he couldn't help smiling.

Katherine smiled, too.

"You're stalling," she said.

"I've never played this for anyone," Bradley said. "I'm a little nervous."

"Well..."

You could make it easier."

"If you say so."

"You won't mind playing for me?" Bradley asked. "An audience of one?"

Katherine shrugged, walked over to the piano, sat down on the bench.

"Schubert," she said. "I love Schubert."

"Of course you do."

"Why 'of course'?"

"He's romantic. Lyrical. A little sad."

"Is that me?" Katherine wondered.

"Yes."

She thought about it for a moment. "You may be right."

She paused and said, "The E flat Impromptu."

It was one of her favorites.

Bradley stood near the piano.

She played the opening delicately, precisely, a rippling stream of notes flowing against shifting harmonies. She moved smoothly into the contrasting second section—more vigorous, more dramatic—then returned to the first theme and the rapid, forceful conclusion.

She waited for Bradley to comment, but he was silent.

"That's all I'm playing," Katherine said and stood up.

Another minute or so passed.

"You have a gift," Bradley said, softly.

Katherine blushed. "Thank you."

He walked over to the piano bench and sat down.

"Another piece in E flat," he said.

"But what about...?"

"Just warming up."

"Bradley..."

"A Brahms Rhapsody."

"Really?" Katherine said. "He didn't break the rules."

Bradley smiled. "You have to *know* the rules before you break them."

"Touché."

He attacked the complex harmonies of the Rhapsody with spirit, caressed the tender melodic intervals gracefully, gave the ominous rumblings a truly sinister tone and finished with a powerful flourish.

"Wonderful," Katherine said.

He stood up. "I need another cup of coffee."

"Bradley!" Katherine complained, but gently.

He went over to the stove and refilled his coffee cup.

"You really are nervous," Katherine said.

"I am."

"Sorry."

"You should be," Bradley said, half-seriously.

"You always seem so..."

"Typical romantic attitude," Bradley said, adding melodramatically, "*I fall upon the thorns of life! I bleed! Nobody hurts like I do!*"

"I don't think I..."

"Everybody's got thorns."

Katherine put her hand on his shoulder.

"Forgive me?" she asked.

"I'll think about it."

"While you're thinking," she said, her hand still on his shoulder, "play your music."

He nodded. He walked to the table reluctantly, put the coffee cup down and returned to the piano. Katherine sat at the table facing him.

He placed several manuscript pages on the music shelf. He looked past the piano, at the fields and the cloudy sky beyond the wall of windows. He began.

The piece opened with a gentle, pastoral theme that, after two repetitions, was joined to a busier, more energetic melody in what became a dissonant fugue. As the pace quickened, contrasting themes and tempos and dynamics were overlaid and woven together and torn apart.

The first time, Katherine had heard only a fragment of the composition and it had sounded chaotic, even frenetic. It was still raw and often discordant, a tapestry of disparate rhythms and harmonies, but she began to sense its structure—how the parts were related to each other. Original themes, familiar popular songs, hymns and folk melodies were all folded into the mixture. The result still made her a little uneasy, but the chaos, the frenzy, had disappeared.

Katherine wasn't surprised by his music this time, but she was still unable to grasp it all. And she was impressed with Bradley's ability to play it. She wondered if she could. She thought she would like to try.

The piece ended with a fierce, harsh cluster of notes.

Bradley looked exhausted. He remained at the piano, his hands in his lap.

"There's a final section," he said. "Brief. Still to come."

He looked at her, waiting for her to say something.

"May I have that cup of coffee now?" Katherine asked.

"Pour me some, too."

She did. He joined her at the table. They drank their coffee in silence.

"Are you being diplomatic?" Bradley asked.

"I'm catching my breath."

"And...?"

They both smiled.

"It's breathtaking," Katherine said. "Not easy to listen to."

"Yes."

"But the logic—I began to hear it."

"You did."

"May I see the score?" Katherine asked.

"When I'm satisfied with it."

She nodded and said, "You played it so well. I don't know if *I* could."

"You could."

"May I hear it again?"

"Not today."

Katherine looked out the window and said, "I could almost see the town. The farms around it. The way a bird might, flying over. Hearing the sounds."

"Yes. Yes."

Bradley leaned back in his chair.

The wall of windows in the studio faced south. Katherine could see a dark, shaggy mountain of clouds moving rapidly north toward her. She heard the warning rumble of thunder.

Bradley saw the fear reflected in her eyes. He reached across the table and clasped her hand.

"Don't run away," he said.

"I can't..."

"Come with me," he said.

Holding her hand, he led her over to the door and opened it, bracing his body against it to keep it open.

"It's moving fast," Bradley said. "Stay here with me. Watch it pass."

Katherine felt the probing fingers of the wind and heard its hungry voice. A flash of lightning was followed a few seconds later by a roar of thunder. She could hear the rain pelting the earth a few hundred feet away, rushing toward them.

"Stay with me," Bradley said.

They were just inside the door, within reach of the storm without being in it. The wind kicked up. The thunder and lightning raced close, closer, overhead.

Katherine could feel the wind's cold, wet breath as the darkness enveloped them. She was shivering. She turned away from the storm, toward Bradley. She embraced him, her face against his chest. He closed his arms around her, holding her tightly.

The storm, the darkness, passed them in a few minutes.

"The sun is out again," Bradley said.

He opened his arms. Katherine turned, looked at the rain-drenched fields glistening in the sunlight. She could still hear the thunder as the storm rode north on the wind.

She pulled away from Bradley.

"I'm wet," he said.

"Me, too."

"Are you all right?"

She nodded.

"Have lunch with me?" he asked. "I can raid the kitchen."

"I—why not?"

"An indoor picnic," Bradley said. "Stay here. I'll be back in a few minutes."

"I hope Matilda isn't too upset."

"Don't worry about her. This isn't her first storm."

As he walked toward the house, Katherine called after him and waved. Smiling, he waved back.

VIII.

During the next two weeks, Boston seemed further and further away. Jamie hadn't answered her last letter. Katherine wondered if fear of the influenza epidemic had driven Amos and the family out of the city.

Louise wrote that she and her husband were keeping to themselves, "just trying to survive. And Simon has postponed his *musicales* until God knows when."

Nell Coogan, Katherine's colleague at the Academy, sent a letter from Maine that reflected the same fear.

There's no need to rush your return to Fielding. Julius has postponed the fall semester indefinitely. From what I read in the newspapers, the situation in Boston is dreadful. The "Spanish flu" is killing hundreds of people. And it's the same in other cities—San Francisco, Philadelphia—and in other parts of the world, too. My God! War and pestilence. "And I looked, and behold a pale horse: and his name that sat on him was Death..." Our sins catching up with us? I'm probably in no danger: I haven't sinned enough!

But Katherine's Kansas life didn't leave her much time to think about Boston.

She insisted on helping Eleanor and Jean Anne prepare (and serve) meals for Duncan and Boyd Richmond and their sons. They were working in the fields from sun-up to sun-down, part of a team of six farm families planting winter wheat on each of their farms. It was exhausting work—the critical first step of the growing cycle.

Katherine still managed to maintain her daily practice routine, and she didn't neglect her students. To Katherine's surprise, Mrs. Grady (of the Bedding and Music Departments) showed the most promise. And sadly, as Katherine had suspected, Emily showed the least.

Katherine also spent more time with Bradley, but she couldn't decide how she felt about him. He was twenty-three—a few years younger than she. That didn't concern her. He was rather handsome, but not nearly as handsome as Jeremy. That wasn't important, either. He was a remarkable talent, and she certainly admired him and enjoyed their time together. And he appreciated *her* talent. But she couldn't forget the way he had broken his engagement and, worse, the way he spoke about it, without sympathy, without regret. Katherine wondered if, despite everything, he was more like his father than he thought.

Bradley had certainly become part of her life, but she wasn't sure how much a part of it she wanted him to be. It seemed to her that he felt the same way: there was no sign of anything but friendship between them.

One afternoon, lunch over and the men back in the fields, Eleanor, Jean Anne and Katherine cleaned the dishes and cutlery and set the table for supper.

"I'm going to lie down for a few minutes," Eleanor said.

Emily was out in the fields with Jean Anne's thirteen-year-old daughter, Margaret, watching (and occasionally helping) the men.

Katherine had planned to practice but Jean Anne said, "I'd like to hear you play."

Taken aback, Katherine looked into her sister's cool, grey eyes, but they were ever a shield of ice on a winter pond, hiding the depths.

"Will you play for me?" Jean Anne persisted.

"Yes, if you like."

They went into Katherine's room—the music room. She sat at the piano and Jean Anne sat nearby.

Katherine was in the mood for Chopin.

Romantic, lyrical, sad? she thought.

She played a nostalgic waltz. A wistful nocturne. And then, for the first time in many months, Jeremy's favorite etude, *Tristesse*.

When she finished the etude, Jean Anne was silent for a moment. Then she whispered, "So beautiful."

Jean Anne had tears in her eyes.

"It is," Katherine said.

The echoes of the music hovered in the air between them.

"When you were a child," Jean Anne said, "when I heard you play..."

"I didn't think you liked my playing," Katherine said.

Jean Anne smiled.

"I didn't want you to know," she said.

"I wish I had."

"I wished I could be like you."

"You did?"

The tears were streaming down Jean Anne's face. She tried to wipe them away.

"You were special," Jean Anne said. "I knew I would always be—what I was."

"I thought..."

Jean Anne stood up and walked toward the door. Her eyes frosted over again.

"I'm so tired," she said, and left the room.

Katherine sat at the piano and listened to the silence.

It was the third week in September. The wheat had been planted and the McKenzies and the other farm families took a deep breath. Now everyone was ready to celebrate at the Haywood County Fair.

During the four days of the Fair, they could look forward to long-winded, patriotic speeches by glad-handing politicians. Revival meetings by Gospel preachers. Exhibits of farm equipment (for sale) and livestock (for sale). Thrilling carnival rides for the children. Lots of tasty foods and drinks (including alcoholic beverages). Raucous brass bands and mournful country singers. Square dancing and a waltz or two. And each day, a race for trotters or pacers.

David and Barbara and other students and teachers from the Agricultural College were going to lead discussions of the latest scientific methods for improving crop yield and quality. President Woodrow Wilson had said, "Food will win the war," so it was a national priority to increase agricultural production, helping to feed America's soldiers as well as our Allies' servicemen and civilians.

And of course there was prize money to be won. Boyd Richmond was certain he had raised a blue-ribbon hog. Eleanor hoped that her special tart-sweet apple jelly would please the judges' palettes. (At the last Fair, her strawberry jam had been virtually ignored.) And although Bradley Munson doubted he and Legato could repeat last year's victory in the featured Haywood Mile, he dreamed of doing just that.

Some people thought the Fair was a bad idea. The Spanish flu had recently struck Camp Funston in eastern Kansas, as well as other army installations in Kansas City, Missouri. Although the cause of the epidemic and how it spread were still uncertain, wherever the disease broke out, public heath officials closed schools and theaters and discouraged large-scale public gatherings. But there were very few civilian cases of the flu in central Kansas—none in the Haywood area—so the mayor decided that the Fair would begin, as scheduled, on the last Saturday in September.

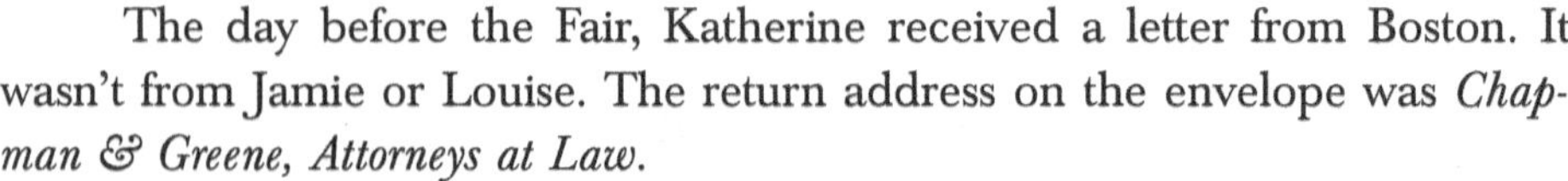

The day before the Fair, Katherine received a letter from Boston. It wasn't from Jamie or Louise. The return address on the envelope was *Chapman & Greene, Attorneys at Law.*

Dear Katherine,

Losing Jeremy was a terrible blow to all of us. Joanna never really recovered. I tried to find some solace in my work but perhaps in the process I neglected Jamie. I warned him to stay close to home, I implored him not to risk mingling with his friends, but he didn't listen. A week ago, he got sick, suffered for three days and died. His mother, who was already in poor health, couldn't cope with another loss. She didn't get sick. She simply gave up.

Only a short while ago, I was content with everything—my family, my life. Now I'm alone. I don't understand why this happened.

I hope you are well.

Sincerely,

Amos Greene

That afternoon, Katherine rode out to the cemetery on the northern edge of Haywood.

Her mother's grave was near her father's, but not next to it. Her father's first wife was buried on one side of him. Roger, their son, was buried on the other side—Roger, who had died at the age of eight.

Katherine's mother was buried next to Roger. As she had requested, her tombstone, unlike the others, made no reference to God or angels. There was only a simple message: her name, the day she was born, the day she died.

Set apart, surrounded by fears, separated from her husband, without a hope of Heaven, she was still lonely in death.

When Katherine returned to the farm, she answered Amos's letter.

Dear Amos,

I wish I could find the right words to express my feelings. You know how much I looked forward to your family becoming my family.

You have my deepest sympathy and my assurance that you are not alone. I hope you will always think of me as your friend.

Love,

Katherine

As she signed the letter, Katherine made a decision: sometime soon she would go back to Boston. But, for the first time, she didn't think of it as going home.

Katherine went to the opening day of the Haywood County Fair with the McKenzies and the Richmonds. They trooped dutifully to the Kansas Aggie School's exhibit, sat through almost two hours of student-teacher lectures (most of which they had heard before from David), tapped their feet to lively country banjos and guitars, watched Emily and Margaret go round and round or up and down on assorted rides, ate ribs and yams and strawberry shortcake, drank apple cider, and watched the judging of the hogs. Boyd Richmond's entry was in the money, but a disappointing third.

Late in the afternoon, just before the trotting race began, the families followed the crowd to trackside. Bradley was already there but, knowing he wasn't welcome, he kept his distance.

"I'll see you later at home," Katherine said to Duncan.

"We can wait for you," he said.

"Don't worry about me. I'll be fine."

She joined Bradley at the rail.

"They're not happy you're with me," Bradley said.

"I wanted to watch the race with an expert."

"I'll do my best to impress you," he said playfully.

"Did you bet on it?"

"I never do, " Bradley said. "My father does, of course."

"Is he here?"

Bradley looked around. "Somewhere. Or maybe Max is doing it for him."

The six sulkies were being driven in tight circles, watched closely by two officials who were at the edge of the track.

"You may remember this," Bradley said.

"Vaguely," Katherine said.

"A 'rolling start.' When the horses are lined up evenly across the track, the starter gives the signal and the race begins."

The sulkies circled once, twice more. The horses came out of the second circle just about even. One of the officials waved a green silk flag and shouted "Go!" And the race was on.

Hundreds of voices were calling the names of trotters: "Magic! Magic!" "Grey Ghost!" "Angel!" "Indiana!" "Sunshine!"

By the time they reached the far turn of the mile track, two of the horses had pulled well ahead and they were neck and neck: Sunshine, a gray stallion, and Angel, a dark bay.

First one would edge slightly in front, then the other would catch up and do the same. As they came down the stretch toward the finish line, Sunshine thrust forward and began to widen the gap.

The bettors who had picked him began to shout his name more confidently.

And then Sunshine broke stride! A roar of disappointment surged over the crowd like an angry wave. It was followed by boos and hisses.

"He gave it away!" someone shouted.

Angel crossed the finish line first, followed by the disgraced Sunshine, whose driver continued slowly around the track, trying to look innocent.

"He was favored," Bradley said. "Angel was a long shot." He laughed. "My father probably bet on him. He's lucky that way."

"You're lucky, too," Katherine said. "I'm going to spend the rest of the day with you."

He took her arm and they walked away from the track.

"Are you in the mood for dancing?" Bradley asked.

"Yes, but I really don't know how to square dance."

"I don't either. We'll wait for a waltz."

"Delighted."

The tent with the dance floor was near the center of the fair grounds.

As they approached it, Katherine stopped and said, "Listen, Brad."

Mixed with the thousand voices of the crowd, they could hear square-dance music from the tent and, off in the distance, a hymn being sung and the rapid-fire ripple of a country banjo.

"Do you hear it?" Katherine asked. "It's your music!"

He nodded. "Yes, it is."

He leaned forward and kissed her cheek.

"Let's find that waltz," he said.

They had to wait for a waltz and they danced it with spirit, if a little awkwardly. They sat out one square dance, then decided to try their luck at another. Unfortunately, despite their sophisticated sense of rhythm, they created a minor crisis and were escorted off the floor.

They patiently awaited another waltz and were rewarded by a long medley that kept them in each other's arms for five or six minutes. They looked around at their square-dance tormentors as if to say, "We do *this* very well, don't we?"

When their triumphant waltz had ended, Bradley suggested refreshments.

"There's cold beer not far from here," he said.

It was a hot afternoon, bathed in a warm south wind. They found shade at a table in the food tent and cooled off with steins of chilled, foamy beer.

Katherine sat close to Bradley.

"I want to ask you something, Brad," she said.

"I haven't finished the score yet," he anticipated. "I still have some work to do on it and—"

"Not about that."

"I thought—"

Katherine leaned closer to him and said, "First, I have to tell you something." She paused and sipped some beer. "I'm not in love with you."

Bradley smiled. "I can believe that."

"I admire you. Your talent. I do."

She put her hand on his arm and added, "And I have—affection for you."

"But you're not in love with me."

"And I don't believe you're in love with me, either?"

"This is a strange conversation," Bradley said.

"Tell me."

"I admire you, too, Kathy."

He took two swallows of beer and smiled.

"And...?" Katherine said, and they both laughed.

"And, although I feel affectionate toward you, I'm not in love with you."

"I have my fears, I know," Katherine said, "but I think *that's* something you're afraid of."

He didn't confirm her observation.

"I just wanted you to know," she said, "that what I'm asking has nothing to do with us being in love."

"All right."

"If we went to your place, right now, your studio. Had a glass of wine. And..." She leaned closer to him and whispered, "...made love..."

He felt her warm breath on his face.

"Kathy..."

"—would I have to worry about—having a baby?"

"I—you mean, do I have—?"

She nodded.

"I'm—yes, I do—you wouldn't have to worry. I go to Chicago or St. Louis now and then and—Jesus, this is ridiculous!"

He leaned back and looked into Katherine's eyes, trying to decide if she was serious.

She wasn't smiling.

"I'm tired of being afraid," she said.

He reached out and touched her cheek with his fingers.

"That's good," he said.

They sat silently for a few minutes, looking at each other, looking away, listening to the chatter of the people around them.

"I didn't come with the family in the wagon," Katherine said. "I can leave with you any time."

"You mean Matilda's going to know about this?" Bradley asked.

Katherine smiled. "She's rather discreet."

"I hope so!"

The cot in the studio was lumpy and uncomfortable; the air, close and tepid.

Katherine couldn't help being frightened. But none of that mattered. Bradley kissed her and caressed her gently, patiently, stroked her hair, cradled her in his arms, until she felt herself responding to him easily, freely.

"I want to tell you something," she whispered.

"Tell me."

"The last night, when Jeremy was going overseas..."

"The last night..."

"When I should have given him something to take with him..." She sighed. "I gave him nothing."

"Kathy..."

"I was afraid. I cried. I didn't give him pleasure. Afterwards, he had to comfort me. Comfort *me*!"

"Was he in love with you?"

"Yes. But I didn't—"

"If he loved you..."

"But he—"

"He understood. Believe me."

Bradley held her tighter.

"Afraid, so afraid," Katherine said.

"Not now?"

Katherine kissed Bradley's mouth, savored the taste of him, the strength of his arms around her.

"Not now."

And later, when the pleasure washed over her, it wasn't about Jeremy or Bradley. She felt that the pleasure was hers, and hers alone.

On the afternoon of the fourth day of the Fair, the featured race—the Haywood Mile for Pacers—was about to begin. Duncan and Eleanor were relaxing in the food tent after she placed second in the jams and jellies competition, yielding first place to Caroline Coolidge, one of the few neighbors she disliked. She smiled at the judges and the victor but quietly vowed to unseat her at the next Fair with a mixed-berries concoction.

David and Barbara were still on duty at the Kansas Aggie tent. Daniel and Emily were with a group of teenagers. When the time of the race approached, the two young McKenzies found Katherine, so they could watch with her.

The three of them managed to clear a space at the rail.

The entry fee for the Mile was $100, and first prize was $2500. Except for Bradley Munson, the competitors were professionals who went from fair to fair, earning a living of sorts. Bradley told Katherine they resented his victory in the 1917 Mile.

"I was an amateur stealing money that should have been theirs," he said. "They won't let that happen again."

"That depends on you and Legato."

"I wish I had your confidence."

Now seven sulkies were circling in the prelude to a rolling start. Bradley may not have felt confident but he looked self-assured as he maneuvered Legato, waiting for the starter's flag to begin the race. The stallion bobbed his head impatiently, eagerly, primed for the competition.

The green flag came down. "Go!"

Someone at the rail, a few feet away, shouted, "*Legato!*"

Katherine was surprised: it was Val Munson. He leaned forward, his arm thrust out, his fist clenched aggressively, and shouted again, "*Legato!*"

Heading into the first turn, Bradley's sulky was one of three slightly ahead of the pack. A smoky gray horse (Summer Wind) was on his right, and a coal-black stallion (Cherokee) on his left. As they made the turn, Legato fell a length or so behind and the drivers of Summer Wind and Cherokee moved closer to each other, blocking Bradley's sulky. He had to pull back on the reins.

Bradley tried to maneuver around the two lead sulkies, but the drivers kept glancing back and smiling as they worked together to stay in front of him. In the meantime, the other drivers edged around them and took the lead.

There were boos and catcalls from the crowd. Val Munson shook his fist. But the drivers paid no attention.

They don't care if they win, Katherine thought. *They just want Brad to lose.*

Their strategy worked. By the time he had reached the far turn, Bradley was too far back to make up the difference. Summer Wind and Cherokee came in fifth and sixth, ahead of Bradley's last-place finish.

"They cheated," Daniel said.

"It looked that way," Katherine agreed.

"We should cheer him up," Emily said.

Daniel frowned. "I don't think we're supposed to talk to him."

"Daniel may be right about that," Katherine said.

"He must feel real bad," Emily argued. "They won't mind."

Daniel wasn't so sure.

In the midst of the debate, Val Munson wove through the crowd and approached Katherine.

"Damn it! He didn't stand a chance," he said, angrily.

"Tell him that, Mr. Munson."

"He doesn't need to hear it from me."

"It'll show you care."

Munson shook his head. "That's not something I can give him."

Now Katherine was angry. "What *have* you ever given him?"

Munson smiled. "He's always known who he *doesn't* want to be."

He turned and walked away.

"What's he talking about?" Daniel asked.

"Never mind," Katherine said. "You have to tell me if you're coming with me."

"Let's go," Emily said.

Daniel shrugged. "Okay."

When they reached the temporary stables behind the track, Bradley and Legato were at a distance from the other drivers and pacers, who were surrounded by admirers. Bradley was all alone, cooling off the stallion with spongefuls of water. He was smiling and relaxed, crooning to Legato, who was obviously upset: "Good boy, good boy."

"That wasn't fair," Katherine said.

"All's fair in love and races," Bradley responded, cheerfully.

"Aren't you mad?" Emily asked.

"I'm not. If they're that afraid of us, we must really be good!"

Katherine agreed. "Now all you have to do is convince Legato!"

Daniel said, "Can I sponge him off?"

"Sure."

Bradley gave Daniel the sponge.

The crowd around the other horses attracted Emily's attention. She edged away from Katherine to get a better look.

"Your father was at the track," Katherine said.

"I'm sure he didn't bet on me."

"He was angry."

"Maybe he *did* bet on me," Bradley said.

"He was angry because of what they did to you."

"That doesn't sound like him."

"I'm certain of it," Katherine said.

"If you say so..."

There was a sudden string of explosions—firecrackers set off by two teenagers in the crowd. One of the horses was so spooked that he pulled free of his driver, reared and ran wild. The crowd scattered and the driver tried vainly to catch up to the horse, which was galloping toward Emily.

Bradley's back was to the scene. Katherine ran past him and picked up Emily, startling the runaway horse again, just enough to make him change direction. His front hoof grazed Katherine's leg, throwing her down with Emily still in her arms. The driver ran past her, in the wake of his horse.

Bradley rushed over to Katherine. Emily was crying but apparently unhurt. Katherine was sitting up, wincing with pain and trying to calm Emily at the same time.

"You're all right, sweetheart," Katherine said. "You're all right."

"Let me look at your leg," Bradley said.

Katherine was wearing denim britches. The cloth over her right calf was torn. Blood was seeping through the tear.

"Anything else hurt?" Bradley asked.

"I'm—I don't think so."

"Come here, Emily," Bradley said. "Anything hurting *you*?"

"N-n-no," she said, still crying. "Just—scared!"

Katherine put her arm around Emily's waist. "So was I!"

"Daniel," Bradley called. "Go to the medical tent and bring one of the doctors back with you."

There were always two doctors on call at the Fair. They treated fairgoers who drank too much, ate too much, or fell victim to some other mishap.

"At least it's my leg," Katherine said. "If I were an organist, I'd be out of luck." She held up her hands. "But all I need is these."

Emily had calmed down. She embraced Katherine and said, "Thank you, Aunt Kathy. Thank you."

"I couldn't let my favorite niece get hurt."

"That was brave," Bradley said.

"The Kansas girl, I guess."

IX.

October was a month for healing. There was a deep laceration on Katherine's leg and a massive contusion around the cut, but the bone wasn't broken. After a week or so the swelling began to subside. Day by day the wound was less painful.

Although the McKenzies were accustomed to the fact that Katherine would never be very useful on the farm, they were proud of her anyway.

October was a month for another kind of healing. The McKenzies invited Bradley Munson into their home.

Duncan said, "We're trying to save David from the draft. Just like Val did. Can't hold that against Bradley. And he's Katherine's friend."

The third week in October David's appeal to the Draft Board was rejected.

The "butcher's bill" for the Great War continued to mount. Victory at St. Mihiel cost more than two thousand American dead and six thousand wounded. In the Meuse-Argonne campaign, more than twenty-six thousand Americans were killed and almost ninety-six thousand wounded.

The specter of war hung over the McKenzie farm like a permanent storm cloud.

One late-October morning at breakfast, Emily announced that she had made an important decision.

"Aunt Kathy," she said, "I've decided to stop taking piano lessons."

"I'm surprised," Katherine said. "You haven't been at it very long. And I think—"

"I love music, but my fingers don't."

"Well, you can still try."

"No," Emily said. "I don't have to *play* music to listen to it."

"That's true."

"And I love to listen."

Katherine nodded. "That's a talent, too, you know."

"It is?"

"Definitely."

Emily kissed Katherine's cheek and said, "I'm very, *very* good at listening."

"I know you are."

"We all enjoy hearing you play, Kathy," Eleanor said.

"Well, I should tell you that *I've* made a decision, too," Katherine said.

"You're going back to Boston," Duncan said.

"Yes."

"You miss the city life."

Katherine looked around the table at her family.

"It's not that," Katherine said. "It's my work. I don't mean teaching. I'll have to do that for a while. The Academy is opening for the Spring Term."

"Is it safe?" Eleanor asked.

"The epidemic there is just about over," Katherine said.

"You said you'll teach '*for a while*.' What then?" David asked.

"What I've been afraid of. The concert stage."

"You'll be famous!" Emily said.

Katherine laughed. "I may not be famous, but I want to try."

"You'll be great," Daniel said.

"You're already great," David said.

Katherine smiled. "Now, if the critics agree with you..."

"When are you leaving?" Emily asked.

"In a few weeks. When I'm completely healed."

"We'll miss you," Eleanor said.

"I'll miss you, too. I'll come back—I'll come *home*—as often as I can."

"We'll keep the piano tuned," Duncan said.

"I know you will," Katherine said.

It was the third week in November, a bitterly cold evening. Katherine was spending a few last hours with Bradley before she left for Boston.

They were in his studio, drinking Cabernet and eating cheese, pretending they were sitting on the flat rock under Bradley's favorite white oak tree.

"Do you love Kansas now?" Bradley asked.

"It isn't love yet," Katherine said.

"Great affection, maybe?"

She laughed. "Maybe."

He reached out and took her hand.

"When I was engaged... She was beautiful and very talented. She loved me. But I didn't love her. For a while, I thought I did."

"Then why did you—?"

"It sounds stupid but she was—she was perfect. What any man would want for a sweetheart. A wife."

"What you did wasn't just stupid," Katherine said. "It was cruel."

"Don't worry about her. She married an architect. An older man. In his late thirties. Rich as Midas."

"I'm worried about *you*. You sounded so—cold."

He kissed her hand. "I'm not cold, am I?"

"No, you're not."

"I never thought I could have what we have. We can be friends—and make love—and just stay friends."

"You never know. We may fall madly in love with each other someday," she smiled.

"I do love you, Kathy."

"I love you, too. But not *that* way."

Bradley took a bite of cheese and sipped his wine.

"You've become a wanton woman, you know," he said.

"I can't deny it."

"A wanton woman who's going to concertize."

"Who's going to try."

"You'll bring down the house."

"I want to do it with your music," Katherine said. "*My Town*."

"That may not be your best option."

"You're publishing the piano version..."

"I'm preparing the score. Should be ready in a week or two."

"I'll learn it. Play it. I know a lot of people in the field. Simon Levin, for God's sake!"

"That's a heavy load."

Katherine nodded. "You should do the same. You must know people. In New York. Chicago. Why not go back to the concert stage? Showcase your work. Mozart did. And Beethoven. Chopin..."

"I get the point."

"You can do what I'm doing. You can try."

"I can try," he repeated, without much conviction.

"I hope you'll visit me in Boston."

"I will."

"You could meet some influential people," Katherine said.

"Like you?"

"Even more influential, if you can imagine that."

"And you plan to come back here?"

"Of course."

"Even though Kansas is too flat?"

"I would call it 'spacious.' Maybe 'too damn spacious'."

"What about the storms and tornadoes?"

Katherine tossed her head back and said, "Challenging."

"Can you hear God singing?"

"Not yet, but I'm trying."

Bradley stood up. "It's getting cold in here."

He walked over to the wood stove and added more firewood.

"I know a much better way to get warm," Katherine said.

She walked over to the cot and sat down.

"A wanton, wanton woman," Bradley said.

She smiled. "And who's to blame for that?"

At the Haywood station the next morning, Katherine was accompanied by the whole McKenzie family. The eastbound train was waiting at the platform.

There were blackbellied storm clouds reaching out from the southern horizon, riding north on the wings of an icy wind. The sun was trying in vain to shed warmth on the Great Plains.

Duncan and his sons carried Katherine's luggage onto the train.

A few days earlier, the Great War had ended. That dark, menacing threat to David had vanished.

Katherine kissed everyone, hugging Emily a little longer than anyone else.

With a heartfelt "Thank you. For everything," she was ready to leave.

"Good luck," Duncan wished her.

"Goodbye, Aunt Kathy," Daniel said.

"We'll see you again soon?" Eleanor asked, hopefully.

"Yes. I promise."

They left the train, waving as it pulled out.

Half an hour into the journey, massive dark clouds overtook the train and a furious hail storm erupted. Ice pellets rattled against the window and pounded the steel walls and ceiling of the railroad car. The wind sang a fierce, angry song.

Katherine smiled, leaned back in her seat, closed her eyes and listened to the storm.

Sweet melodies stir dreams of love and visions of Heaven. But no matter how sweet the song, one must ask, "Who is the singer?"

The Food of Love

If music be the food of love, play on...
                    —Twelfth Night, Shakespeare

Fin-de-siècle Vienna, in the turbulent years before the Great War, was a simmering, seething political cauldron: an archaic Austrian Emperor and his effete courtiers stubbornly clung to the last vestiges of imperial power, besieged by the nationalistic fervor of Serbs, Croats, Bosnians, Herzegovinians, Hungarians. Despite the political turmoil—or perhaps because of it—the intellectual and artistic life of the city flourished. Vienna's vibrant coffeehouse culture embraced such remarkable men as Sigmund Freud, Ludwig Wittgenstein, Gustav Mahler, Stefan Zweig and Arnold Schönberg—revolutionaries all.

In the Viennese musical realm, the unchallenged sovereign was the violin virtuoso Maximilian Solange. His technique was flawless. His tone, his interpretation, his insights were unmatched. As was his range: he commanded a vast repertoire, from the earliest Baroque concerti to the latest atonal excursions.

Born in Aix-en-Provence in the south of France, he was the only child of a prosperous merchant. When he was a boy, his mother, a talented amateur musician, taught him privately. As a teenager, he studied at the Conservatoire de Paris and completed his studies there in just three years. "They could teach me no more," he said.

After graduation and before he settled in Vienna, Solange toured Europe for four years, applauded enthusiastically by the critics and the public.

In short, Solange was the master of his art. Other violinists envied him and spoke of his artistry as they had once spoken of Paganini's: "He must have sold his soul to the Devil."

To which Solange replied, "I didn't have to sell my soul. The Devil has already claimed it for his own."

Even his most ardent admirers acknowledged the truth of that remark. For although his music seemed divine, in his personal life he was an unashamed hedonist, a sexual predator, seeking pleasure and offering it, but never love or respect. Now in his late thirties, as his artistry grew in brilliance, his sexual appetites pushed further and further into the dark side of passion.

One restless spring evening, Solange felt the telltale pangs of ennui that he always felt when he began to tire of his latest conquest. In this case, a twenty-year-old painter named Elisabeth. She had been more difficult to seduce than most. But, like the others, she had succumbed and, like the others, she was no longer of interest to him. After all, it had been almost a week.

They had just returned to his apartment from dinner. Elisabeth sat close to him on the sofa, her soft hip pressing against him. She was anticipating a passionate evening of lovemaking.

Solange poured the champagne.

He raised his glass and said with a smile, "To Elisabeth: a farewell toast."

She looked puzzled. "Are you going somewhere?"

He finished the contents of his glass with one swallow and refilled it.

"No, my dear," he said. "You are."

"But, I..."

"I have plowed the same field too many times."

"But you said you loved me."

"Weren't you warned about me?"

She looked down, tears beginning to flow and said, "I thought with us it would be different."

"It *was* different. For a day or two. But one must move on."

"*Move on*? Have you no shame?"

"None at all. I'm sure you have enough for both of us."

She stood up, whispered, "Damn you!" and left.

Solange shrugged and drank another glass of champagne.

He repeated, under his breath, "One must move on."

A few minutes later, Elisabeth not even a memory, he was walking toward the Café Schindler with his violin case under his arm.

It was a beautiful evening. The sun was just a pale glow in the west. Swarms of diamond-bright stars were beginning to speckle the dark, cloudless sky. A fresh breeze stroked Solange's face.

"Who will she be?" he wondered.

And already he could sense the excitement of a first kiss, a first touch.

"Who will she be?"

When he entered the café, the maître d' bowed to him and said, "Herr Solange, we are honored to welcome you back. It has been too long."

"Thank you, Karl. I suppose someone else is sitting at my usual table."

"Give me a moment. I will settle the matter."

True to his word, Karl quickly returned and led Solange to a table next to the bandstand.

"I will bring a bottle of your favorite *schnapps*, Herr Solange. On the house, of course."

As he drank, Solange was greeted by some men and women who knew him, or wished they did. He exchanged a few words with them, examined the women, but found none that he fancied.

"Who will she be?"

He had finished half the bottle when Karl reappeared, bowed and asked, "Do you think... Would you favor us...with a melody or two?"

Several people seated close to Solange murmured, "Yes," "Please."

Solange nodded, opened his violin case and drew out the instrument and the bow. The crowd spontaneously applauded.

He rose and was about to climb up to the bandstand when a woman stepped in front of him. She was almost as tall as he. She wore a black, loose-fitting dress—simple, almost stark, certainly not fashionable—and a black hat with a black veil that covered her face. She held out a sheet of music in a gloved hand and said, "I wrote this for you. Play it for me."

Her voice was throaty and sensual.

He smiled. A woman of mystery. A new challenge. A new kind of conquest.

"With pleasure," he said, taking the sheet from her and stepping up onto the bandstand.

She sat at his table, folded her hands together and waited.

The music, written in ink on staff paper, was titled "The Food of Love."

Solange scanned the notes quickly, tuned his violin and began to play.

At first, many of the people in the café continued to talk or laugh or order more drinks. But after he had played five or six bars the crowd grew silent. Even the waiters stood quietly and listened.

"The Food of Love" was a slow, subtle stream of melody with a velvety tone Solange had never heard before, even from his own violin. As note followed note, arching through the air, he felt the music touch him deeply where he had never been touched before. And as he played, he watched the veiled woman and his hunger for her grew stronger and stronger. He couldn't see her eyes, but he knew she wanted him the way he wanted her, more than he had ever wanted any woman. When he stroked the final chord of the piece, his mouth was dry, his heart was beating fiercely.

He didn't hear the crowd's applause. He came down off the bandstand, put his violin and bow in the case and said to her, "Come with me now. To my apartment."

He heard her laugh, a low sultry laugh.

She rose. He put his arm around her waist and pulled her close.

As they left, the crowd applauded again, cheering another of Solange's conquests.

When they entered his apartment, he put the violin case down with haste.

"No, no," she coaxed. "Play the piece again while I get ready."

It was dark in the apartment but she told him she wanted to make love in the dark.

"Play," she said. "Do you remember it? 'The Food of Love'?"

He nodded.

"Yes, yes," he said. "I could never forget it."

And as he played, she began to undress.

The melody mesmerized him, caressed him, aroused him. He played it more feverishly, with bolder strokes.

And then she was naked. The hat and the veil were gone.

"This is for all of us," she whispered.

She was a female. But she wasn't a woman. And when she had finished her lovemaking, all that remained of Maximilian Solange was his violin.

The Legend of Jean-Paul LeBeau

There is a little truth in every legend. How much truth is there in the legend of Jean-Paul LeBeau? That, you must decide for yourself.

In the middle of the sixteenth century, in Anjou, on one of the lazy branches of the Loire, was a quiet little village called *Île de Rêves*—the Island of Dreams. If you visit this village today, you will discover that it is not an island at all. It sits snugly on a peninsula. But its citizens insist that long, long ago, the river embraced Île de Rêves in its watery arms. And who are we to argue with them?

You may ask, what were the dreams dreamed in this village long, long ago? Alas, those dreams have been forgotten.

In this region of France, Henri, *Le Comte de Villeneuve*, a loyal subject of King Charles, was the local monarch. The Count of Villeneuve owned virtually all the land and took the lion's share of the harvests. He also owned all the mills and wine presses and took his fees for their use. In return, he offered his protection—and his protection was sorely needed. This was a turbulent time when, all over Europe, Catholics and Protestants shed their blood in an endless struggle for power. The Count and his troops kept the village safe.

In fact, he had a special affection for Île de Rêves: when the Count's young son lay dying from a terrible fever, *Père Alain*, the parish priest, had prayed at the boy's bedside day and night for weeks on end, and the child had miraculously recovered. The Count was a man of faith. He believed that the priest's prayers had saved his son's life. And so he rewarded Père Alain by ordering the installation of a magnificent organ in the village church. To house the instrument, the church had to be rebuilt—enlarged and refurbished—and the Count was delighted to pay for it all.

Père Alain, a humble and, truth to tell, a rather simple old clergyman, dared not take pride in the new church and its wondrous organ: that would have been sinful. In fact, the Count's gift soon became a source of embarrassment to the priest. Although the church was now much larger, the congregation wasn't. The worshippers tended to crowd together at the front of the nave, as if they feared the rows and rows of shadowy, empty pews behind them. And the voices of the choir and the flock echoed strangely, eerily in the hollow chamber.

But for Père Alain, that wasn't the worst of it. Now that the church had an organ, who would play it? The deacon, Albert, sang like an angel, conducted the choir with enthusiasm and played the lute. But not the organ. Indeed, there was not an organist to be found in Île de Rêves or any of the villages around it. The choir (and the congregation in its responses) had always sung the Mass without accompaniment. Who would summon the mighty voices of the great organ? No one, it seemed.

Bishop Rocher, a stern, scholarly cleric with a reverence for tradition, heard reports about Père Alain's "new" church, and traveled from Angers to inspect it. He was not pleased.

"The Count has bestowed what I can only call a *dubious* gift," the Bishop said to Père Alain. "Your village church is *absurdly* large now. It has outgrown its congregation. And the organ? Does it offer more to God than plain chant or a reverent harmony of *human* voices?"

"It does not," said the priest, sadly.

The Bishop frowned. "Should we add *flourishes* to divine worship? Make the Mass more *theatrical*? More *operatic*? Less *holy*?" His eyes flared in anger. "Perhaps we should even abandon Latin and pray in French!"

As the priest knew, the Latin Mass had been forcefully reaffirmed by the Council of Trent not long ago—in stark contrast to the Protestant translation of sacred texts into the vernacular.

Père Alain bowed his head and muttered, "*Mon Dieu!*"

The Bishop's visit left the priest in an agitated state. Day after day, Père Alain stared at the great, silent organ pipes, the untouched keyboards and pedals of the mighty instrument, and sighed with despair. He prayed meekly for God's help.

Then one warm, humid August evening, Jean-Paul LeBeau appeared.

It was the hour before Vespers. Père Alain was at the altar, watching the organ intently, as if he feared it would suddenly start playing itself.

He heard the rapid click of boots behind him. He turned and saw a tall, slender young man approaching, hatless, a black cloak wrapped around his shoulders.

The young man walked up the steps of the altar. The priest turned to meet him.

The stranger's long hair was the palest shade of blonde. His face was bloodless and unlined. His gray eyes were as cold as winter ice, as proud as a stallion.

"Père Alain, I am Jean-Paul LeBeau," he said. He formed his words tentatively, as if he were trying to remember a forgotten language. "I have come a long way to Île de Rêves. To play my music for you. For your church. For your flock."

He leaned down and whispered to the priest, "Listen, Père. Listen."

His breath was as chilly as a December wind.

He moved past the priest, tossed back his cloak, and sat down at the organ.

"Listen," he said again.

His hands and feet attacked the keyboards and the pedals, slowly at first, but gradually gathering speed. His body swayed rhythmically from side to side, faster and faster. And for the first time, the silent organ sang. A river of melody flowed across the altar and burst into the empty nave—a flood of passionate music, a torrent of voices high and low, vibrating, twisting, turning, thrusting apart, intermingling. Melodies the priest had never heard before.

Père Alain marveled at the beauty, the passion. The waves of sound washed over him, sensuous, seductive. He trembled, swept up in a whirlwind of emotion.

"Is it the passion of *faith* I feel?" he wondered. "Or the passion of the flesh?"

He couldn't tell the difference, and that frightened him.

LeBeau played for almost an hour, tirelessly, fiercely, filling the empty church with his thrilling music, filling Père Alain with a troubling blend of fear and exaltation. Suddenly, after a thunderous, thrusting, climactic chord, the organ fell silent. LeBeau leaned forward, seemingly exhausted, his head almost touching the keyboard. Père Alain sighed and tried to calm the rapid beat of his heart.

He heard muted voices behind him and turned to see clusters of his parishioners, sitting in the pews, standing in the aisles. The music had drawn them into the church. Their faces reflected the priest's confused feelings.

LeBeau stood up, wrapped his cloak tightly around his body and came to Père Alain.

"May I add my music to your..." (he hesitated here) "...worship?" he asked, his voice barely above a whisper.

Père Alain said, "You may."

LeBeau nodded. "I shall begin tomorrow."

"Albert, the deacon, will work with you."

LeBeau turned to walk away.

"Wait, Monsieur LeBeau. Do you have a place to stay? We must..."

"The cobbler, Pierre, lives alone. His wife died quite recently, quite suddenly. He will have room for me."

"But we cannot presume..."

LeBeau put a long, thin finger to his lips and said, "We can. I will see Albert tomorrow morning, after *Matins*."

He walked slowly down the aisle, past the murmuring congregants, out of the cool darkness of the church and into the sultry August heat.

In the days and weeks that followed, LeBeau surprised Père Alain and Albert by his willingness to support the choir and the congregation with musical ornaments that were both restrained and subtle. As word of his talent spread throughout the region, the congregation grew to fill the church. The collection boxes were stuffed with contributions. The priest was pleased, but still uneasy.

Le Beau remained cold, distant, always keeping to himself. When he wasn't at the church playing the organ, he stayed in his tiny room in the cottage of the cobbler, Pierre.

"He has no life except for his music," Pierre observed.

"So it seems," Père Alain said.

Then one day, LeBeau made a suggestion: "Perhaps, now and then, I could play some of my own music—a recital—for my own pleasure. Nothing profane, of course."

"Of course."

"And if the villagers wish to attend, so be it."

"So be it."

And so it was. Between the services, from time to time, LeBeau would find an hour for his music. At first, Père Alain avoided these solo performances. But he couldn't stay away. Neither could most of his congregants. And as the word spread, the recitals attracted people from all over the region.

The priest knew that LeBeau's music—the music he created—was certainly not holy. But was it merely secular, or was it profane? That was a thornier question, and it tormented the simple priest on many sleepless nights. But in truth, LeBeau's melodies were so beautiful, so inspiring, that Père Alain was willing to live with that paradox.

He went so far as to send a letter inviting Bishop Rocher to one of LeBeau's recitals. (By now, the organist's performances were scheduled weeks in advance.) The Bishop responded by demanding a private recital. Of course, Père Alain agreed.

Autumn had come to Île de Rêves. The green trees of summer were shedding leaves of red, brown and gold. Warm breezes were turning into chilly winds. And the Bishop's mood matched the weather.

He stood with Père Alain at the altar, arms folded across his chest, eyes narrowed. For a moment or two, LeBeau faced them with his back to the organ, as if he were protecting it. Then he bowed slightly, turned and sat down, throwing back his ever-present cloak and leaning forward to play.

The organ's many-throated voice began to swell, to soar, melodies rising and falling, intertwining, arching. The Bishop listened, his expression unchanged. But as the music filled the nave, he closed his eyes, swaying to the rhythm. Père Alain nodded, smiled, sharing the Bishop's pleasure. LeBeau's melodies embraced them both.

Suddenly the Bishop shook his head, opened his eyes and whispered, "No. No. No," softly but angrily.

He rushed down the steps of the altar to the font of holy water. He gathered some of the water in his cupped hands and ran up the steps of the altar, past the priest to the organ. He threw the holy water at LeBeau. There was a brilliant flash of light, a muffled scream and LeBeau disappeared, leaving behind the last echoes of his music.

Père Alain covered his eyes with his hands. When he uncovered them, the Bishop was at his side, a half-smile on his face.

"Don't be afraid, Père," he said. "Our faith is strong."

"Yes, Your Excellency."

"When I was first ordained, twenty-five years ago," the Bishop said, "there was an organist at Notre Dame de Paris, a young man named Jean-Paul LeBeau. His talent was extraordinary. We were captivated by his music. We should have known better. For he was a sinner. A fornicator. A spawn of the Devil. The archbishop excommunicated him and drove him from the sight of decent men. And in the company of sinners, he died."

Père Alain crossed himself. Twice.

"Satan has sent him back to tempt us once again," the Bishop said.

Père Alain crossed himself again.

"We may sleep, Père, but Satan never does."

Père Alain bowed his head and kissed the Bishop's hand.

"I shall never forget that, Your Excellency. Never."

"*Deo gratias.* Thanks be to God."

"*Dei gratia.* By the grace of God."

Père Alain never again let Satan catch him unawares. But on a summer night, now and again, as he looked up at God's shining carpet of stars, he remembered the haunting, seductive melodies of Jean-Paul LeBeau. And, perhaps, in his long, holy, humble life, that was his only sin.

The only thing sadder than a dream unfulfilled is a dream undreamed.

The Messenger

It was the fortieth autumn of my life. The coldest autumn. The loneliest.

At work, I watched others, less talented than I, move up the corporate ladder. My boss said that I had gone as far as I would ever go. "You should have paid more attention to your career, less to your job."

I had been living with Marie for more than three years but, day after day, we had less passion, less to talk about, less to share, until love was barely a memory. We didn't even kiss when we said our final goodbye.

After she left, I fell into a quietly numbing routine: dinner at a coffee shop near my apartment, or an Italian restaurant on Seventh Avenue; walking for an hour or so; maybe a couple of Manhattans at a tavern on West 84th Street. Then going home and trying to fall asleep.

On weekends: a glass of wine or two or three; a book, a movie; a baseball or football game on television. And no interest in finding another Marie.

And I prayed.

God and I have had an uneasy relationship. I grew up in a Jewish home, where religion was an obligation, never a joy. My grandparents lived with us. They had come to America from a small town in the Czarist Ukraine. For them, God was dangerous, unforgiving. When my grandfather smiled, he covered his mouth with his hand. He was afraid that God would think he was too happy and send misfortune his way. A heavenly pogrom.

My parents performed the rituals. They attended services occasionally during the year, always on the High Holidays. I went to Hebrew School and was bar mitzvahed. But as far as I knew, my parents never asked God for anything or expected anything from Him.

I didn't share their God. I had my own. Not dangerous or unforgiving. Not Jewish. Or Christian. Not anyone else's. He was someone I could talk to. Someone who could understand me. Although He never answered me, I was sure He was there.

I kept up our one-sided conversation, even when my marriage fell apart, when downsizing cost me my job, when my mother died and my father married a woman I despised.

I believed God was listening to me because things got better. I found another job—maybe not as good as the one I lost, but not bad. I found Marie, maybe not as exciting as my wife, but smart enough and attractive.

I got the message. He was there.

Now, in my fortieth autumn, I needed Him again. I prayed. I waited.

On my evening walks, I sometimes browsed at Bauer's, one of the last surviving second-hand bookstores in the city. It was long and narrow, a dimly-lit literary catacomb—two floors of crowded shelves, roughly divided into Fiction (most of the first floor) and Non-Fiction (all the rest), which in turn was categorized as Ancient History, Erotica, Americana, Photography, et. al.

I've never cared much for fiction. Detective stories, occasionally. Most often, it's history (any period) or science that interests me. (When I was in college, I thought I would become a biochemist, but mathematics discouraged me.)

The owner, Mr. Bauer, was a desiccated Dickensian character who said he had owned this bookstore for almost fifty years. He sat on a high stool at a desk at the rear of the first floor, reading, ignoring customers until they approached him to ask a question or make a purchase. He was stoop-shoul-dered, dusty, his thick white hair like snow on a dark mountain.

One evening, as I grazed the Geography shelf, I found a massive *Atlas of the World* covered in thick leather, its pages gilt-edged. According to the title page, it was printed in 1910 in Boston.

I love maps. Old maps particularly, because they are time machines. They show you the world that used to be.

Was this a rare book? More than I could afford?

I asked Mr. Bauer.

"Estate sale," he said. "Syracuse, I think. Cost me almost nothing."

He took the atlas from me, hefted it, groaned at its weight, studied it for a moment, handed it back to me and said, "Ten dollars."

Before he could change his mind, I pulled the bill from my wallet. He rang up the sale on the cash register, gave me a receipt and immediately went back to his book.

I returned to my apartment, more hopeful about the evening ahead. Settling down at the desk with a glass of Cabernet, I began a journey to the turn of the Twentieth Century, a time of stagnant monarchies, vast colonial empires, simmering rivalries, shifting alliances.

When I reached *Asia*, I found a few sheets of yellowed paper crushed between the pages of the book—a kind of manuscript tied together with a loop of twine. Hidden there, perhaps.

I examined the manuscript, seven large sheets written on both sides in black ink, the handwriting bold and sharply slanted. It was a letter.

Autumn, 1908

Mrs. Anderson,

My name is Joshua Daniels. You may remember me. You were my teacher many years ago when I was only ten. You taught me to find "treasures in books." That's what you said. Thanks to you, Mrs. Anderson, I still find those treasures.

Yours was the last class I ever took. The next year my grandparents kept me out of school. I had to stay on the farm, away from town, away from other children, away from other people. They were ashamed of me.

I'm writing to you because I remember the way you taught me and I think you'll understand. And if you're still teaching, maybe you'll want to tell your students what I'm telling you. Not my story but what I've learned.

My mother and I lived with her parents on their farm. It was far from town, in the shadow of Tanner's Mountain, in the shadow of what my mother had done. I'm sure you heard the story. I often did. My grandmother repeated it over and over again to me with the same words, in the same rhythm, almost like a song, an angry song.

"Lucas came to help us that Spring, when Grandpa hurt his back, when he couldn't do much work. Lucas was a young man, tall, strong as a bull...big smile, soft voice...handsome, *too* handsome. Came from nowhere, stayed for two or three months, went back to nowhere. Left your mother with you in her belly. Went back to nowhere."

When I was very young she would stroke my hair with her heavy hand and look deeply into my eyes, not to soothe me, but to frighten me.

My grandfather lived virtually in silence, his spirit numbed by years of endless, grinding toil. He listened to his wife's sermons but didn't hear them. When I was old enough I helped him. The crops, the hens, the cows, the pigs gave us just enough to live on year to year. No more than that. We were hungry sometimes.

I don't remember my mother. Grandma said she was weak, couldn't survive, didn't live more than a year after I was born.

"It wasn't your fault she died," Grandma said, "it was his fault. He came from nowhere, went back to nowhere."

But I knew she blamed me.

At school I didn't make friends. I didn't need friends or want them. I wasn't used to being friendly. And they all knew about what my mother had done. They didn't treat me badly. Because I was tall and strong like my father, they didn't bully me. They ignored me. I got used to being alone.

I had a hard time learning. Most teachers gave up trying. You didn't.

Grandma said school didn't matter anyway. School didn't feed the pigs, didn't plow the field. She read to me from the Bible, words I couldn't understand. Strange names, strange stories. She said the Bible was truer than anything they taught me in school.

"The war never ends," she warned, "the war between the angels and devils fighting for our souls."

She would chant the verses, blurring the words, "And the beastwhichIsaw was like unto a leopardandhisfeet were as thefeetofabear and his mouth as the mouthofalion..."

She hunted sin and fed on it like a righteous lioness.

When I was ten you were my teacher, Mrs. Anderson. I think you cared about me. I don't know why. You taught me to understand. To think. It was the best year of my life until then.

But when I was ten it started. My body began to change. It happened slowly. At first, the first year, we didn't notice it. Then it seemed to happen much faster. The bones of my chest grew larger. Curved more. Made my chest broader. And my shoulder blades grew too, pushing out the skin on my back.

There was no pain but I was terrified. What was happening to me? What did it mean? Was I becoming a monster? A freak?

I couldn't sleep on my back anymore. I would lie on my belly in bed in the middle of the night and listen to the voices of insects and birds and animals in the dark. And I would moan and cry and shiver with fear.

But then, after a time, I wasn't afraid. On the contrary. The new bones and muscles seemed natural to me.

Not to Grandma.

"Angels and devils," she said, "angels and devils."

On my eleventh birthday she told me I wasn't going back to school. That I couldn't ever go into town again.

"Only God knows what you've become," she said.

"I'm your grandson."

She frowned.

"What was your father? Angel? Devil? Only God knows."

Now she and Grandpa never touched me. They looked at me out of the corners of their eyes as if I were unspeakably ugly.

I didn't feel ugly. And as my body grew and changed month after month I felt a mysterious hunger, a hunger that I couldn't name.

My wings had begun to take shape. They were small at first, covered with my skin—new parts of me that I could move as easily as I moved my hands and legs.

I had to cut openings in my shirts.

Grandma and Grandpa fed me. Watched me. He worked. She prayed.

I read the Bible. Read about angels. In *Genesis* when Abraham was going to sacrifice his son Isaac an angel stops him:

> *Lay not thine hand upon the lad, neither do anything unto him: for now I know that thou fearest God, seeing thou has not withheld thy son, thine only son from me.*

In *Exodus* God sends an angel to Moses:

> *Behold, I send an Angel before thee, to keep thee in thy way, and to bring thee into the place which I have prepared.*

In *Matthew*:

> *In the end of the sabbath, as it began to dawn toward the first day of the week, came Mary Magdalene and the other Mary to see the sepulcher.*

My chest grew larger. My wings grew longer and much stronger. And now I was sure I knew why.

Was my father a messenger? Was I a messenger? A messenger of God?

Yes, I thought. That was why I was different, why I was alone. That was the reason. That was my purpose.

I only had to wait for His message to come to me.

I began to wander in the hills beyond the farm. They were canopied with the foliage of massive trees as far as the eye could see. In summer it was cool and shady there. In winter the ruthless cold bit deeply and the icy winds froze you to the bone.

There was a little pond a mile or two from the farm where ducks and frogs and snakes lived and predator and prey came down to the water to drink. Sometimes the predator hovered in the shadows, poised to kill, like a latent sin hiding in the darkest places of the soul.

I learned to fold my wings tightly across my shoulders. Grandma sewed me a cloak that would hide them. Grandpa built a shed behind the barn where they could hide *me*. I ate and slept there. It had a fireplace to keep me warm in the winter.

I spent more time in the woods. I ate wild fruits and nuts that I gathered. Sometimes I came back to the farm just to sleep.

For more than a year I lived that way. I was at home in the woods. In the wilderness with all its savage honesty, I could be me. To the other creatures I was just one more potential enemy, so they watched me but they didn't judge me.

And when the day came—the day I felt that strange hunger again—I knew what it was.

I went into the hills, climbing to the highest point on the highest hill, hundreds of feet above the woods. I took off my cloak. I looked up at the sky and then down over the edge of the hill.

I unfolded my wings. They were very long and wide now, strong, ready. The muscles in my chest and shoulders moved them quickly up and down and then faster and faster. I took a deep breath, my massive chest swelling. It was time.

Shaking off my fear, I stepped back a few feet, then ran forward off the edge of the hill into the air. I began to fall. I tried to scream but the breath was sucked out of me. Desperately, I flapped my wings—and suddenly I stopped falling. I was pushing at the air, rising higher and higher, closer to the sky—like Icarus, closer to the sun.

That first flight, I was aloft for only a few minutes. I flew back to the top of the hill and landed too hard, twisting my ankle. But I didn't stop. I had to learn everything. How to turn, how to rise and fall slowly, how to land without breaking my legs. I kept at it, over and over again, hour after hour. Up and down. Learning how to use my wings. Learning how to fly. How to see the world the way eagles see it.

And then I slept. I dreamed that I touched the moon with my fingertips.

A few days later, I knew that I could no longer live on the farm. I told Grandma and Grandpa I would never come back. She argued for a while but I could see she wanted me to go. I told them not to worry about me. I don't think they did.

I had found a cave many miles from the farm in a place that could be reached only through the air. At night I took what I needed from the general store in town—oil lamps and tools, dishes, pots and pans—and carried them to my cave. I took clothes and shoes, too. Surely not a sin if I was fulfilling my destiny.

I cut wood in the forest and built a room with a floor and walls and I built a chair and table and bed. I punched a hole in the roof for a chimney and made a fireplace out of bricks. I made mistakes and had to do things over but after many months my home was finally finished.

I was only fourteen years old but I was already full grown at over six feet tall. I could fly for hours because I had learned to glide, letting the wind carry me in its invisible hands. I flew in every direction, as far as I could—north and east and west and south, over forests and lakes and farms and cities—soaring on the currents in the cold thin air. Birds changed their flight paths to avoid me. Even eagles and hawks stayed out of my way. Sometimes I chased them through the sky. And there were times I touched the wet mist that was the clouds.

I saw the world the way no other man had ever seen it unless there were other men who were also angels.

I was lonely. Of course I was. But wherever I traveled, and I traveled far, I never met another like myself.

And I waited for His message. Month after month. Year after year.

I knew that someday I would become His messenger.

The world beneath me kept changing. I grew older. The years passed and still I waited.

I had grown up very quickly and I have grown old just as quickly. I am not yet forty but my muscles are weary and my bones ache and my vision is failing. I can't fly as long or as high as I used to. I get weaker every day. I know that I am dying.

Last night I flew to the top of the tallest hill and gazed at the night and the moon and the stars. And I finally accepted the truth, that He will never send me a message. Because there are no messages from beyond. There may not be a beyond. The only messages are from within.

I don't know why I became what I am. My father may have carried a seed of the past, a time before history, when there were people like me in the world. Angels. Devils. Giants in the earth. Maybe that's what all the legends are about.

But that doesn't really matter, does it? Whatever I am, it was up to me to rely on myself, to make the most of myself, here in this world, right now. That's all anyone can do. That's my message.

It's true that I was lonely, Mrs. Anderson, but please don't feel sorry for me. *I have soared with eagles!*

Your student,
Joshua Daniels

Rising from the desk, I slipped the letter back in its loop of twine, returned it to its hiding place and closed the old atlas.

I walked to the window and looked up at the star-speckled night sky. For a moment, I imagined I could see the shadow of Joshua Daniels' wings against the face of the full moon.

It was the fortieth autumn of my life. The coldest autumn. The loneliest. But I was never again as cold or as lonely.

The Boarding House

Adler moaned, hugging his shivering body with his thin arms, trying to remember, trying to forget. Unable to do either.

The television set in his room flickered in the darkness, a noisy night light flashing scenes of exploding bombs, marching armies, chanting crowds, burning cities. And every so often, a face filled the screen—an angular, jagged, brutal face, dark-browed, dark-eyed, fiercely proud and without mercy.

The radio in Adler's room played a constant stream of trite, sentimental music. It was a vulgar, dissonant counterpoint to the sound of the television set.

He hadn't slept. He never slept. He was always too cold, or too hot. Sometimes, without warning, the landlord would turn up the heat in the boarding house—fierce dry heat that seared Adler's lungs.

From cold to heat to cold to heat. There was no pattern, no way to predict it. And no middle ground.

How could he sleep? The cold, the heat, the flickering light of the television screen, the radio music. And always, the sounds of pleasure next door in Karen's room, where she and Karl enjoyed each other. And always, down the hall, the endless arguments between Mr. Bloomberg and his wife—he shouting, she whimpering.

How could he sleep? How could *anyone* sleep?

He wanted to scream, to vent his anger, to hurt someone. He wished he could. For a moment, he almost remembered what it was like to shout, to hurt someone. Almost.

He was hungry and thirsty. He would take a shower and go downstairs to the dining room for breakfast.

He pushed the covers away and got out of bed. The naked, wooden floor was smooth and cold against his bare feet, like a sheet of ice. He had no slippers. He opened the door of his room and walked down the hall to the bathroom, shivering, coughing.

He took off his night clothes, folded them carefully and placed them on the closed lid of the toilet seat. In the full-length mirror on the wall, he examined his image: gaunt sallow face; narrow slender body, flaccid, weak.

But when he looked into his own eyes—*only* there—he saw the distant, angry echo of another time.

He stepped into the bathtub and moved the selector lever to "Shower." Instantly his body was stabbed by searing hot needles of water. The sudden shift from cold to hot left him dizzy and gasping, but he didn't move.

The bathroom door opened. Karen and Karl came in. They usually did. She pulled the shower curtain to one side. She was naked. She was exactly the kind of woman Adler had always desired: icy gray eyes and long red hair; plump and fleshy body, wide-hipped and white-skinned.

Karl was wearing a bathrobe. He was tall and muscular. He stood behind her, his arms around her, feeling her breasts, caressing her belly, holding her close to him.

Karen's eyes inspected Adler's body.

She said, "He's quite a specimen, isn't he, Karl?"

Karl laughed.

She leaned toward Adler, ran her hand over his sunken chest and his withered thighs, and then between his thighs, touching, stroking, rubbing.

Adler felt the hunger for her, the ache for her. It burned inside him, like the needles of water that scalded his flesh. He remembered the touch of sex, the taste, the tension. But the yearning was trapped inside him, behind a wall of steel, and he couldn't reach it.

Karen laughed and said, "Still can't get it up, Adler? Poor little thing."

She turned in Karl's arms and they kissed and caressed each other.

Looking back over her shoulder, she laughed again. "Poor little thing," she taunted as they left the bathroom.

He dried himself with a towel that was stiff and abrasive and went back to his room to dress.

Downstairs in the dining room, breakfast was on the table. He took his usual seat opposite Karen and Karl. (Now, she was wearing a bathrobe, too.) Mrs. Bloomberg sat at Adler's left, and Mr. Bloomberg to *her* left, at the head of the table.

The television set on the sideboard flashed scenes of marching soldiers, mob violence, hurricanes and tornadoes. The radio beside it played a constant stream of banal, sentimental music.

The scrambled eggs, as always, were cold. The toast was burned and coated with rancid butter. The coffee was lukewarm and weak. As always. And mealtime was always breakfast time.

For a few moments, Adler remembered: breakfast had been his favorite meal—chilled orange or grapefruit juice; stacks of hot pancakes dripping with butter and sweet syrup; omelets swollen with cheese and ham and onions and mushrooms; croissants torn open and smeared with thick marmalade; strong, sugarless, black coffee. Linen napkins and tablecloth, fine china and silverware. Whispering servants, soft music in the background, and a beautiful, red-headed woman smiling at him from across the table.

The memory disappeared, leaving a vacuum behind it. And at the table, across from him, Karl and Karen whispered to each other and kissed and fondled each other's bodies, and laughed at him.

Karen smiled at Adler and mouthed the words, "Poor little thing."

At the head of the table, Mr. Bloomberg shouted and frothed about World Events, waving his newspaper in the air like a dull, paper sword. And at Adler's side, Mrs. Bloomberg sobbed to Adler about her "lost opportunities" and touched him, tentatively, with her cold, bony hand.

He ate everything on his plate and drank his coffee. He always did. It didn't matter: he was always hungry and thirsty.

He went into the parlor. The television set flashed images of war and devastation. The radio played Viennese waltzes.

He took the book from the table, sat on the sofa and read it again.

"No man was ever more powerful, or more dangerous. No man was ever responsible for so much death, so much suffering. No man was ever less repentant."

Adler looked up at the television screen, at the proud, brutal face of the man he was reading about.

Adler thought, "He said there was no such thing as 'sin.' There was no God. There was only life and death, and there was nothing beyond death."

Adler looked away from the television screen. His eyes searched for a window, forgetting that there were no windows in the boarding house. For all he knew, beyond those walls was Paradise itself. Or its darker mirror image.

Closing the book, he stood up, stared at the face on the television screen for a few minutes, and then returned to his room.

He closed the door behind him, but he couldn't lock it.

Sometimes, Karen and Karl came in and taunted him.

Sometimes, Mrs. Bloomberg came in, and pleaded for his attention and his sympathy. He gave her neither.

He sat down in his chair. In the darkness, the television screen flashed images of marching soldiers and rioting crowds. The radio played maudlin, romantic music.

Adler thought, "If only once, just *once*, I could break through the walls and let my anger and my lust and my hatred pour out of me. Just once.

"There was a time, I remember, when I would merely nod my head and cities would burn, and civilization itself would tremble. I walked across the map of the world like a giant, crushing everything under my feet.

"There was never a man more powerful, or more dangerous, or responsible for so much death, so much suffering. Repentant? But it was such joy!"

He wished he could say those words, but he couldn't speak. He, who could rouse an audience to fury and revenge, couldn't speak. He raged inside, but he could say nothing.

He didn't know what it was like for anyone else. He didn't even know if there *was* anyone else. He was sure that the other boarders worked for the landlord.

The landlord. He was clever. *Damned* clever.

For Adler, there were no flames, no torture. He was small, weak, and powerless. Ridiculed. Angry, but mute. Lustful, but impotent.

How long had he been at the boarding house? He didn't know. How long would he be there?

How long is forever?

Goldman the Jeweler

A sweltering July morning in 1932. An apartment on Essex Street on the Lower East Side of Manhattan.

Goldman the Jeweler awoke at 5:30 as he did six days a week, a half hour before the alarm clock rang. He was a thickset, homely man in his mid-forties, with a broad face and restless, dark-brown eyes.

He looked down at his still-sleeping wife Esther. Although she was only thirty-five, the beauty of her face had eroded, along with the energy of her youth. He felt not even the memory of affection or passion for her.

He showered, shaved and dressed in a dark blue suit, white shirt and tie. By the time he had finished, Esther, in a shapeless bathrobe, was preparing breakfast for him and their nine-year-old son, Isaac. She would eat later.

"Finish your cereal, Isaac," Esther said, in a weary voice, as if reciting a prayer she knew wouldn't be answered. "You won't grow if you don't eat."

He was a slender boy, small for his age but aggressive.

"I want a bagel," Isaac said, "like Daddy."

He glanced at his father for approval.

"If you finish your cereal..." Esther promised.

Isaac shrugged his little shoulders and picked at the cereal, while Esther cut a bagel in half for him and covered it with cream cheese.

Goldman wasn't impressed by Isaac's act of defiance. Children didn't interest him. He could picture himself, knife in hand at the altar, a new Abraham, willing to consummate the sacrifice of his son.

He finished his coffee.

"Time to go to work," he said.

He kissed his wife on the cheek, kissed his son on the top of the head and left.

Goldman walked to his store every morning—a fifteen-minute walk down Grand Street to Second Avenue, where he bought a copy of *The Daily News* at the corner newsstand. Then two blocks up Second to GOLDMAN'S FINE JEWELRY.

Originally, it had been MESSER'S FINE JEWELRY, owned by Esther's father. Twelve years ago, Goldman had gone to work for Sam Messer, a widower with one child and a diseased heart. Goldman soon became Messer's indispensable right arm and Esther's husband. Two years later, Messer had succumbed to a heart attack, Esther inherited the store and Goldman changed the sign.

Messer once said, "You got a perfect name for a jeweler. Diamond is good. Or Pearl. Or Silver. But Goldman is better. You're not the product—the *gold*—you're the *man* who sells it."

Messer had also said, "Honesty is the most important thing for a businessman. Without honesty, you're finished—down the toilet."

Goldman the Jeweler thought honesty was overrated.

Goldman turned off the alarm with a key, opened the store and switched on the lights. He walked down the main aisle into the back room where there was a large, rectangular safe. Against the side wall was a coat rack, a cot, a sink and a miniature single-burner gas stove complete with a blackened coffeepot.

Goldman hung his jacket on the coat rack and loosened his tie. He wiped sweat off his brow with his index finger.

In a couple of minutes, the coffeepot was simmering over a low gas flame. Goldman opened the safe. He took a steel box from the top shelf and caressed it with his thick fingers. He opened it and studied its contents: three stacks—one each of ten-, twenty- and fifty-dollar bills—bound tightly with rubber bands. He touched them, fondled them, smiled, closed the box and returned it to the shelf. Then he began to transfer bracelets, rings, brooches, necklaces and watches into the store's display cases. He worked quickly, efficiently, in the rhythm of a well-practiced ritual. When he had finished setting up the jewelry, the coffee was ready. He poured himself a cup and carried it to the work table in the rear of the store. He turned on the fan facing the table and sat down to read the newspaper.

It was 7:45. He didn't open for business until 9:00.

The news wasn't good. These days, it never was.

The front-page story: On President Hoover's orders, General MacArthur called in the Army to kick the Bonus Marchers out of Washington, D.C. They were veterans of the First World War—thousands of them—who had come from all over the country demanding immediate payment of a bonus they had been promised. It was supposed to be paid in 1945, but they said what everyone knew: times were hard. They couldn't get jobs. They were desperate. They camped in and around Washington in tents, lean-tos. Some had even been allowed to camp in abandoned government buildings scheduled for demolition. But finally Hoover decided he couldn't afford to pay the bonuses now. The Bonus Marchers had to leave. The Army made sure of that. It was a bloody scene. "Tragic," said the newspaper.

Goldman had served in the army in 1918, but was hospitalized with pneumonia right after basic training. By the time he was healthy enough to go overseas, the war had ended.

Everyone wants something for nothing, Goldman thought. *I don't need a goddamn bonus. And where the hell would the money come from? From people who pay taxes. People like me.*

At 8:15, someone began knocking repeatedly, nervously, on the back door of the store. Goldman wasn't pleased. He drank another mouthful or two of coffee, stood up slowly, and walked just as slowly through the back room to the door.

It was Mike Wells.

"I got somethin' for you," Wells whispered, patting the breast pocket of his shabby jacket.

"You look like hell," Goldman said. "Come in."

Wells was tall, narrow-shouldered, furtive. He pulled a necklace out of his jacket pocket. It was a gold chain with a row of half-carat diamonds interrupted by a larger, deep-blue sapphire.

"Beautiful, huh?" Wells said.

Goldman took the necklace and said, "Wait here."

He went to the work table in the shop, examined the gems carefully through a loupe, took another sip of coffee and returned to the back room.

"Fifty dollars," he said.

Wells frowned. "Jesus Christ!"

Goldman's expression didn't change.

"Fifty dollars," he repeated.

"Jesus Christ! It's gotta be worth a coupla grand."

"You don't know how much it's worth."

"I gotta have more money. I need it."

"That's old news."

"It's gotta be worth a lot."

"It's worth nothing if you can't sell it."

"Jesus Christ!"

"I don't think He's going to answer you," Goldman said softly.

"What?"

"Never mind. Okay, I'll make it sixty."

Wells' eyes narrowed. "Son of a bitch," he whispered.

"You're paying me for a service," Goldman said. "I can move this piece for you. I know the right people. And remember, the cops never bother me. So they don't bother you. Right?"

He gestured for Wells to follow him to the table. He opened the petty-cash drawer and counted out sixty dollars.

His back was to Wells. He sensed a sudden movement and turned quickly. Wells was a few steps away with a switchblade knife in his hand. Goldman dropped the money, reached behind him under the top of the table and pulled out a three-foot length of lead pipe.

"Come on," Goldman said. "I'll break you in pieces, you fuckin' coward!"

Wells grimaced, edged forward, the knife held out in front of him.

"I'll bust up those hands of yours," Goldman said. "There goes your whole fuckin' career. Right?"

Wells hesitated, sighed, clicked the knife shut and put it away. He held out his hand.

Goldman pointed to the floor and said, "Pick it up."

Wells got down on his hands and knees and picked up the money.

"Get the hell out of here," Goldman said.

After Wells left, Goldman locked the back door.

He smiled.

These days, the jewelry store wasn't making much money. Fortunately, his other business was doing very well.

Minnie, Goldman's sales clerk, was late this morning. She arrived fifteen irritating minutes after he opened the store.

He had tightened his tie and put on his jacket.

"I don't like you being late," Goldman said.

"I couldn't sleep last night," Minnie said softly. "It was so hot. I wasn't feeling well."

She was a slim, dark-haired, dark-eyed woman in her early twenties.

He reached out and pressed his heavy palm against her forehead for a moment.

"You got a fever?" He laughed sarcastically. "Sit at the table, by the fan. You'll cool off a little."

"Thanks."

She sat down, enjoying the electric breeze, and watched as Goldman parked himself on the table near her.

"So you couldn't sleep last night?"

She nodded.

"The heat doesn't bother me," he said.

"You're lucky."

"You make your own luck."

"Maybe so."

"Nobody gives you anything," Goldman said. He raised his hand and closed his fist. "You got to *grab* it."

"I guess..."

He leaned toward her and said with a sardonic smile, "But you got to pay the price."

She waited for him to continue, knowing what he was going to say, what he always said.

He pointed his index finger at his heart.

"I had to marry Esther."

Minnie closed her eyes for a moment. When she opened them, Goldman had leaned even closer.

He studied her angular face, her thick dark hair pulled back in a tight bun, her deep-set eyes shaded by thick lashes.

"I don't—*want* my wife," Goldman said. "You know that."

"I'm...I can't..."

He stroked her hair, touched her cheek the way he had touched the stacks of bills in the safe.

"But at least, we have..."

"Mr. Goldman..."

His hand followed the line of her neck down to her shoulder, which he caressed roughly. He pulled her to her feet, toward the entrance to the back room, toward the cot in the back room.

"Mr. Goldman..."

"We have each other. Right?"

"I can't today. My period."

Goldman shrugged, touched her mouth and said, "We'll make do."

At a few minutes after 4:00, Detective Sergeant Sean Kelly came into the store. He tipped his hat to Minnie and walked to the work table where Goldman was replacing the clasp on a thin gold bracelet.

"Sergeant Kelly, what a pleasant surprise," Goldman said.

He put down the bracelet and leaned back in the chair. He clicked the fan's motor onto "high" and it began to whine like a spoiled child.

"Hot as hell," Kelly said, removing his hat.

Goldman smiled unpleasantly. "That's where we'll be someday. Better get used to it."

"I might try for a suspended sentence. If I can find me a priest when my time comes."

Goldman shook his head and said, "I guess that's how the church holds onto people."

"It's never too late to convert."

"God and me, we don't see eye to eye."

"You're not—afraid?"

Goldman thought a moment. "I worry about today. Tomorrow. Not the day *after* tomorrow."

"I'll tell you what I'm worried about *today*," Kelly said.

He moved closer to Goldman, turned to be sure that Minnie was still at the opposite end of the store, and said, "One of your—friends—may offer you an item that—well, you shouldn't touch it."

"An *item*?"

"A necklace. Diamond and sapphire."

"What's the story?"

"It belongs to the wife of the Chief's best friend."

Goldman laughed.

"It's no joke. The Chief is really pissed off."

"Makes him look like a fool."

"He wants blood," Kelly said.

"I can't spare any."

"There's lots of pressure."

"Lots of pressure."

"Don't screw with it, Goldman. You could get hurt."

Goldman pointed a thick index finger at Kelly. "You wouldn't let me get hurt, would you?"

"I...It's not my call."

"It better be."

"I can't..."

Goldman wagged his finger. "If I get hurt, you'll get hurt."

"Listen, I'm just trying..."

"*You* listen. Keep me out of trouble—like always—and I'll keep feeding your pension fund."

Kelly put on his hat.

"You are some rotten son of a bitch."

"That's old news, Kelly. Old news."

Minnie left at 5:00. Goldman was in no rush to go home. He emptied the display cases, put the jewelry back in the safe and locked it.

A handful of customers had come into the store that day. A young man bought his fiancée an inexpensive engagement ring—an unadorned gold band clutching a tiny diamond.

He apologized to her about the price and said, "Someday, honey, I'll buy you the moon."

She may have believed him, but Goldman didn't.

A weak sister, he thought. *Apologize to a woman and she's got you by the balls.*

Goldman had enjoyed the visit of an Uptown lady, who arrived in a limousine. She walked into the store tentatively, cautiously, as if it were enemy territory.

She's here to sell, not buy, he thought. *And she can't do it in her neighborhood. She's got to keep up appearances.*

Goldman took great pleasure in haggling with her, ignoring her hostility, answering it with arrogance, and buying some fine pieces at bargain-basement prices. He put those pieces in a large velvet sack that he kept on the bottom shelf of the safe. He once told Minnie it was his "off-the-books" shelf. She knew what that meant.

At a few minutes after 6:00, someone knocked at the front door. It was Jessica, the sales clerk Goldman had fired last November.

He unlocked the door.

"Can I see you a minute?" she asked, eyes cast down deferentially.

He shrugged, motioned her in and closed the door behind her.

Jessica stood just inside the doorway, leaning against a display case as if for support. She was a plump, awkward woman in her early thirties.

She brushed a coarse strand of pale brown hair from her eyes and said, "I thought...I wondered..."

"You thought? You wondered?"

"I've had a hard time."

"Can't find another job?"

"I did. For a few months. But..."

Goldman nodded and said, "You didn't know when you had it good. Right?"

"I didn't know."

"You had a decent job."

"Yes."

"The work wasn't that hard."

"It wasn't."

He thought for a moment, remembered the soft flesh of her thighs, her breasts, her belly. But he remembered more than that.

"You're sorry you left?" he asked.

"Yes. I'm sorry. I wondered..."

Goldman smiled. "Wondering again?"

"If I could come back..."

"Come back?"

"Part-time even."

"Part-time?"

"I need..."

"I know what you need," Goldman said. "But you're not what *I* need."

Jessica clasped her hands together, raised them, as if in prayer.

"I'm sorry. What I said."

"You're sorry."

"I was—upset..."

"So was I," he said.

Jessica pressed her hands against her breast and said, "Anything you want...I'll do..."

Goldman pointed a thick index finger at her.

"So Jessie will do *anything*," he said.

"Anything," she whispered.

"But you said I was 'disgusting.' 'Immoral.' A 'monster.'"

"I was—I was—"

"Upset."

"Upset," she echoed, softly.

"I have a clerk who's doing a good job. She's cleaner than you. Younger. Prettier."

"If you could—"

"You're nothing to me. That's what you'll always be."

He opened the door and said, "Get out. Again."

Her eyes flared with anger for a moment, but the flame died. She left the store. He locked the door.

The next morning at 9:35, Minnie and Detective Sergeant Sean Kelly were in the back room of the jewelry store looking down at the body of Goldman the Jeweler.

"This is how you found him?" Kelly asked.

"Yes."

"What time was it?"

"A little before nine."

"The alarm was off?"

"Yes."

"Was the door unlocked?"

"Yes. And the back door was open."

Goldman was lying face down on the floor. There were several deep, bloody gashes on his head. A bloodstained pipe lay beside him on a towel.

"That's his 'weapon' isn't it?" Kelly asked.

Minnie nodded. "I checked under the work table. It's his."

Kelly leaned over the body, examining it more closely.

"The blood's still a little wet," he said. "It happened this morning."

"I called you as soon as I saw—him."

"Did you touch anything?"

"No."

Kelly walked over to the safe.

"It looks like the jewelry—most of it, anyway—is still here."

Minnie pointed. "He kept a lot of money in that box. Money's gone."

"How much?"

"I don't know."

"But why is the jewelry still here?"

"Maybe he got scared. When I came in."

"Or maybe he doesn't know how to fence the stuff."

Kelly walked around the body, studying it from every angle.

"He was hit three, four, five times," he said. "On the *back* of the head. The killer didn't face him. Sneaked up on him."

Minnie nodded.

"You got an inventory, so we can check if any of the jewelry was stolen? It must be insured. His wife's gonna need the money."

"I'll give you the books he kept," Minnie said. "His wife owns the store. At least she has that."

"She can hire somebody to run it."

"Sure."

"Maybe you?"

"No. I won't stay here."

"You gotta make a living."

"I have—something—lined up."

Kelly studied her closely for a minute. She seemed calmer, more relaxed than usual. He wondered if she was strong enough to swing a lead pipe.

"I should tell you, Sergeant, that not everything is listed in Goldman's book."

"Why not?"

"Goldman kept some pieces separate. He called them his 'off-the-books' pieces."

"Are they still here?"

"Yes. In a sack on the bottom shelf."

"Have you seen any of them?"

Minnie shook her head and said, "The insurance company doesn't know about them."

Kelly nodded.

"Nobody knows about them."

"You do."

Minnie smiled. "I never heard of them."

Kelly paused. Then he smiled, too.

"I don't expect to find any fingerprints—except his," Kelly said. "And yours, of course."

"Of course."

"Whoever did this—the towel was wrapped around the pipe so there wouldn't be prints on it."

He looked at the safe and said, "The money can't be traced."

"His wife will be better off," Minnie said. "She still has the store."

"Yeah."

"And I guess the police will take care of those off-the-books pieces."

"That's right. I'm gonna call the lab guys in a few minutes."

"Would it be all right if I go home? To calm down."

"Yeah."

"I could come to see you at the station later today. If you want me to go over everything."

"I'll be there this afternoon."

Minnie started to leave, but stopped and asked, "Do you think you'll catch the killer?"

"I doubt it," Kelly said. "And you'd be surprised. In a couple of weeks, this'll be old news."

How bittersweet is love remembered. And, oh, how sad is love forgotten.

Final Arrangements

Early on a Tuesday morning in May, Abel Pritchard began to make his final arrangements.

The early morning had always been his favorite time and, even now, at seventy-seven years old with a pacemaker intermittently adjusting the rhythms of his heart, Abel still awoke at 6 a.m. every day. After breakfast he took his usual walk downtown on Fifth Avenue, from his apartment on 88th Street to Central Park South. It was more than two miles.

He was a tall, slender man, who still walked with an athletic stride—almost a swagger—his shoulders back and head high. But these days he had to stop for an occasional rest on a park bench.

Before he retired (at the age of sixty-eight), his walk would end at his office—Pritchard & Reese, Architects—on 54th Street. Now he might walk down to the pond for a few minutes and sit there watching the water, or tracking the choppy, nervous flight of a passing sparrow or pigeon. Then he would start back uptown, usually through the park, following one of the paths that led him home.

Although this morning began no differently than most, something unusual happened. Passing the Metropolitan Museum of Art he saw his partner and best friend, Samuel Reese, coming toward him across Fifth Avenue. Even out of the corner of his eye, before he saw Sam's face, Abel recognized his walk: feet pointed out awkwardly, shoulders slouching, eyes looking down at the sidewalk or up at the sky. Sam was in his late twenties, a short, already-balding, slightly overweight young man who wrinkled a freshly-pressed suit the moment he put it on.

Abel stopped in front of the Museum and called out Sam's name.

Sam smiled at him and said, "Abel! I didn't notice you over there."

"Too busy dreaming up new projects?"

Sam laughed.

Abel said, "It's nice to see you again, Sam. It's been too long. I'm walking downtown. Care to join me?"

"Sure, sure."

After they had walked for a minute or two, Sam pointed at the leaf-heavy trees.

He said, "The city is beautiful this time of year, isn't it? In the spring, everything seems possible."

"Why would anyone want to live in Miami or Los Angeles, or anyplace that doesn't have seasons?" Abel wondered. "A year should measure your life like a clock, season by season: birth—death—rebirth."

"Abel, I can't believe it. You've become a poet in your old age!"

"Well, I have more *time* to be poetic."

"So you're not on your way to work?"

"No, Sam. I left the firm quite a few years ago."

"Did you do everything we planned? Did you change the world, even just a little?"

"Not even just a little."

"That's too bad. When we started out, you were more of a dreamer than I was. You said, 'We're going to change the shape of architecture! We're going to throw away the rule book. No, better than that: we're going to write a *new* rule book with a thousand new options—a thousand new possibilities. And when we're finished, the world will look different because of *us*—Pritchard and Reese.' That's what you said."

"That's what I said."

"We did some beautiful things in the beginning. The Kirkwood School downtown. One critic called it, 'Urban light and shadows.' Remember?"

"Yes."

"Or the Fairchild Center in Seattle, reflecting the clouds and the rain and the mountains?"

"Yes, Sam, I remember. But you can't limit yourself to projects like that—to clients who give you all that freedom. There aren't enough of them to keep a business going."

They passed a homeless man sleeping on a bench, wrapped in a stained blanket. A shopping cart filled with odds and ends was parked alongside him.

Sam recalled, "When we were still in school, you had this idea to work with city governments, designing a new kind of homeless shelter. Simple, functional apartment buildings with street-level shops and restaurants that would employ the tenants, so they could earn a living."

"Young ideas. Not every problem has a solution."

"We might have been able to pull it off."

"We were going to *donate* our services, right?"

"Right."

"That's good for the city, and bad for the architect."

"It could be good for the soul."

Abel said, "The dreams of youth."

Sam shook his head.

"They weren't just dreams, Abel: They were a new vision."

"Sam, life isn't *The Fountainhead*. The real world was a lot tougher than we thought it would be. You've got to pay the bills."

"Yes. Pay the bills."

"You never cared about money, did you, Sam?"

"Never."

"But you only had yourself to worry about. I had a wife, a son—"

Sam gave Abel a sly look: "And a *lifestyle*, too?"

"I guess you could say that."

"And before we knew it, the passion had disappeared and we were just like everyone else."

"You should have gone out on your own, Sam."

"I'm a *follower*. You were the one with the real talent, with the courage. I couldn't do it by myself."

"Maybe you could have."

Sam didn't answer.

After a beat, Sam asked, "Did Gillespie take over the firm?"

"Yes."

Sam studied the sidewalk carefully. He said, "I never liked him."

"He did a lot of networking, made a lot of contacts. He attracted some big clients."

"So you started to design shopping malls? And big, swollen mansions for people with loads of money and no taste?"

"That's what we did, Sam."

"But the price was right?"

"Yes."

They walked in silence for a few minutes.

Then Abel said, "Could we sit down? I get a little winded."

"Sure."

"Maybe, if you hadn't left me so soon, we could have done some of those things. Maybe..."

Sam shook his head. "My death just gave you the excuse you needed, Abel."

"That's true. I lost the vision. I stopped caring. Other things became more important."

Abel paused for a moment, then added, "But there's something I want you to know. Toward the end, just before I retired, I told Gillespie I was taking over a major project: the design of a new hospital in a suburb of Minneapolis. I did all of the work myself. I looked at the possibilities the way you and I used to. I even imagined talking to you about it."

Sam grinned warmly. "I hope I came up with some good ideas."

Abel nodded.

"It's a beautiful building," he said. "Comfortable, functional, welcoming, *organic*. (Wasn't that your favorite word?) It's the kind of place you would be proud of."

Sam's eyes glistened.

Abel said, "I just wanted you to know that I came full circle. I came back to where we began."

"Thank you, Abel. That's good to know. We left some beautiful things behind us, didn't we?"

"Yes, we did."

Sam stood up and said, "I've got to be going. Nice to see you again."

"Goodbye, Sam."

Abel watched him walk away.

He continued his morning walk going south on Fifth Avenue for a few more blocks, then turned onto a path leading into the park.

His wife was standing in the cool shade of a massive oak tree, waiting for him. Helen was in her early forties, still slim and attractive. But the line of her mouth was already too tight, and there was no forgiveness in her eyes.

She said, "What am I doing here? We have nothing to talk about."

"I wanted to see you one more time."

"Why? To remind yourself that our marriage was a failure?"

"No. To understand why."

"That's easy. Too much romance. Too little reality."

"But you wanted the romance, didn't you?"

He tried to see her twenty-year-old face behind the mask of her forty-year-old impatience. He couldn't.

She winced. "Romance. Beauty. Passion. For a while, I was young enough to imagine that's what I wanted. But only for a while. I grew up."

"Is that what happened?"

"Yes. It took you a lot longer."

"Those first few years, I couldn't believe how lucky I was. I had everything I ever wanted."

"That's because you dreamed the wrong dreams," she said.

"I won't argue with you now. We've had enough of that."

"What *do* you want?"

"I want to know if you ever really loved me."

"I suppose I did. You were handsome. You seemed to be ambitious. You were a lot smarter than me. I knew you'd be successful."

"That doesn't sound like love."

"What the hell *is* love? It isn't poetry, Abel. That wears pretty thin, pretty fast. I'm too practical for all of that. I always was."

"When I saw you the first time, I thought, 'That's the perfect design for a woman. I couldn't have done better myself.'"

She frowned and said, "There's that damn poetry again."

"Being a mother didn't matter to you, either, did it?"

"I'm not the maternal type. It's an instinct I never had."

"I don't think I ever got to know Robert. Someone else was always taking care of him. Nannies, tutors. Then he was away at school. Then he was gone."

"Accidents happen."

"That's all you can say about our son?"

"Remember, Abel, *he* was an accident, too."

"Yes. Of course. The only thing our marriage produced was a mistake."

"You were still young enough when we got our divorce. You could have found someone else, I'm sure. Or designed one. A new dream girl."

"No. I didn't trust myself anymore. I never had another relationship that lasted very long. I made sure of that."

"And, of course, it's all my fault."

"No. I used to blame you for what happened. That wasn't fair. You didn't fool me. I fooled myself. That's what I wanted to tell you."

"You've told me. May I go now?"

"There's just one more thing. The girl I married wasn't someone I imagined, was she? Wasn't there at least a part of you that was like her? That loved me?"

The line of her mouth softened a little, and there was a hint of forgiveness in her eyes.

She sighed, "Maybe. It was so long ago."

And slowly turning, she walked away.

He followed a winding path toward the pond. Alisha Robbins was sitting on a waterside bench. She was twenty years old, a slender, delicate young woman, with honey-colored hair and dark blue eyes. Abel sat down next to her. She reached out and took his hand in hers.

"How have you been, Abel?" she asked.

"I'm still here," he answered, smiling.

"I hope you've had a good life."

"Some good times, some not so good."

"The world catches up with us," she said.

"In the beginning, the possibilities are unlimited. At least you think they are."

"We did."

"You were going to be the next great American poet."

"I was just one of many," she said. "A few books. An occasional review. Barely a ripple."

"I read all of your work."

"You did?"

"I wish I really understood it."

She laughed. "At least you tried."

"You know me: I'm terribly prosaic."

"Architects are dreamers, too."

"*Practical* dreamers. Steel and glass, not similes and metaphors."

"That's a nice phrase. A little practical poetry."

He smiled. "There were times when I read your poems, I could hear your voice. I remember the way you read them to me. I loved to listen to you."

"You were my first audience."

"You made me feel the rhythm, the flow, the music of it."

"I'm so pleased that you read my work. I didn't have a lot of fans."

He studied her face for a moment or two.

"Alisha, you're just as beautiful as I remember you."

"But not beautiful enough to marry."

Abel shook his head.

"That's not why. I want you to know why I didn't ask you to marry me."

"You said you weren't ready. You still had a lot of schooling ahead of you. And you didn't think it was fair to make me wait."

"That's what I said."

"But it wasn't the reason?"

"No. I was afraid."

"Of me?"

"Of disappointing you. Of failing you. I didn't think I could live up to what you thought I could be. I want you to know that."

She raised his hand to her lips, kissed it and said, "You shouldn't have worried about failing me, but about failing *yourself*."

Abel nodded.

"Yes. Of course."

He stood up.

"It was wonderful seeing you again."

Alisha smiled and said, "I think I'll sit here for a while. It's a lovely day. Goodbye, Abel."

"Goodbye, Alisha."

He was getting tired now, walking more slowly. He couldn't seem to absorb the freshness of the air or the warmth of the sun.

He followed a circular path near the pond toward a stone bridge. Standing on the bridge, watching the clouds stream across the sky, was Abel Pritchard, seventeen years old. A tall, gawky boy, long-armed and narrow-hipped, with most of his joys and sorrows still ahead of him.

Abel joined him on the bridge.

"Good morning, Abel," he said to the boy.

"Good morning."

"Mind if I bend your ear for a few minutes?"

The boy shrugged.

"I got a feeling you're going to talk about the good old days," the boy said. "That's what old men always do."

Abel smiled and said, "Not this old man. I just want to tell you a couple of things I've learned."

"Okay."

"Whatever you do, whatever choice you make, you could have made another. But it might not have been better."

"What if it *was* better?"

"Might-have-beens don't matter. If you caught the one that got away, it would just be another fish."

The boy shrugged. "If you say so."

"Time moves too fast. You think you have years ahead of you. But it seems like only seconds before all the possibilities become memories."

"Seconds," young Abel whispered.

Abel put his hand on the boy's shoulder.

"I did the best I could. I want you to know that. I wish it could have been better. Goodbye, Abel. Good luck."

"Thanks," the boy said.

Abel left him on the bridge and started to walk back home.

The morning sun grew brighter and warmer. The streets became more crowded with traffic and people. But despite the heat of the sun, Abel felt the numbing cold of January creep into his body, touching him deeply, chilling his blood, freezing his breath, stroking him like an icy hand, until the cold was all there was.

Mary Anne

A One-Act Play

Characters:

The WIFE, *a soft-spoken, patient woman in her seventies.*
The HUSBAND, *a nervous, aggressive man in his seventies, whose memory is
    dying.*

Time:

The Present. An April morning.

Setting:

*The screened-in porch of a lakeside summer home in Connecticut. A small folding
    table and chairs downstage center.*

At the Curtain:

The WIFE *is seated at the table, drinking coffee and reading a newspaper. She
    looks relaxed. She reacts to a story in the newspaper, smiling, shaking her
    head. The* HUSBAND *enters, hurriedly, unsmiling.*

WIFE. Good morning, dear.

HUSBAND. Morning.

(He looks around aimlessly for a moment, focuses on the table, walks over to it and sits down.)

WIFE. It's a beautiful day.

HUSBAND. Beautiful?

WIFE. Look at the sun on the lake.

HUSBAND. Hurts my eyes.

WIFE. The sky is clear. Not a cloud anywhere.

HUSBAND. What month is it?

WIFE. April.

HUSBAND. April?

WIFE. Yes.

HUSBAND *(Under his breath, tentatively).* April showers...bring...bring...

WIFE. May flowers. That's right, dear.

HUSBAND. Can't have showers—without clouds. *(He laughs, a short, sharp laugh)* No clouds? Guess it isn't April.

WIFE *(Smiling).* It's one of those rare cloudless April days. *(After a couple of beats)* Would you like some breakfast, dear?

HUSBAND. Ummmm...

WIFE. Coffee? *(He nods. She pours him a cup).* I could scramble some eggs.
Fry up some bacon.

HUSBAND. I don't like eggs. Hate eggs.

WIFE. You used to enjoy scrambled eggs.

HUSBAND. I hate eggs!

WIFE. All right, dear.

HUSBAND. I want something sweet. A muffin. Toasted. With butter.

WIFE. Fine.

HUSBAND. Yes, a muffin.

WIFE. I'll make it for you.

HUSBAND. That's what I want.

(WIFE *walks offstage left.* HUSBAND *drinks coffee. He picks up the newspaper,
riffles through the pages, stops and reads an item. He looks up from the
paper, puzzled, squints as if he's trying to remember something, throws the
paper down on the table.)*

WIFE *(Offstage).* I'll be back in a moment.

HUSBAND *(Under his breath).* April showers...May flowers. Showers. Bring
flowers. *(Loudly)* Goddamn it!

WIFE *(Offstage).* What did you say, dear?

HUSBAND. Nothing.

WIFE *(Enters, carrying a muffin on a dish. She puts the dish in front of him,
kissing him on the forehead).* Something sweet for you.

HUSBAND *(Stares down at the dish)*. Something sweet. *(He takes a bite of the muffin, drinks some coffee)* Molly is sweet, isn't she?

WIFE. Yes, she is.

HUSBAND. She's our daughter.

WIFE. Yes, dear.

HUSBAND. A sweet girl.

WIFE. Very sweet. *(After a beat)* But a grown woman now.

HUSBAND. She's a young girl.

WIFE *(Cautiously)*. That's the way you—the way we remember her. Of course. But she's forty years old. Has children of her own.

HUSBAND. Of her own?

WIFE. Michael and Jennifer. Our grandchildren.

HUSBAND. I don't like the boys she goes out with.

WIFE. You never did.

HUSBAND. She's too good for them.

WIFE. It seemed that way, didn't it?

HUSBAND. She gets mad when I tell her. *(Laughs)* Boy, does she get mad!

WIFE. That's Molly all right. Sweet and mad.

HUSBAND. One of these days, she's going to get married.

WIFE. She *is* married, dear.

HUSBAND. So young and married already?

WIFE. She's not a little girl anymore.

HUSBAND. Not anymore.

WIFE. She married Robert. She met him when they were going to college. UConn.

HUSBAND. Yukon? Alaska?

WIFE. The University of Connecticut.

HUSBAND. Robert. Tall, thin. A teacher, right?

WIFE. That's right, dear. They live in Ridgefield.

HUSBAND. Not far from here.

WIFE. A half-hour away. We were there a couple of weeks ago.

HUSBAND. What did I think of Robert?

WIFE. You liked him. He may be the only one you ever liked.

HUSBAND *(He smiles)*. But she married him anyway.

WIFE *(Nodding, pleased with his humor)*. That *is* funny!

HUSBAND. Are they happy?

WIFE. Yes.

HUSBAND. I wonder...

WIFE. What do you wonder?

HUSBAND. There must be happy marriages.

WIFE. Of course there are.

HUSBAND. Most marriages are unhappy.

WIFE. Why do you say that?

HUSBAND. It's true.

WIFE. I don't think so.

HUSBAND *(Thinks for a moment)*. Our son. David?

WIFE. Yes. David.

HUSBAND. Unhappy marriage.

WIFE. I'm afraid so.

HUSBAND. A very unhappy marriage.

WIFE. Very unhappy.

HUSBAND. He never did anything right.

WIFE. He was a good student. Very smart.

HUSBAND. Was he?

WIFE. Yes. Honors classes. Always one of the best.

HUSBAND. I don't remember that.

WIFE. We were proud of him.

HUSBAND. Does he live in Ridgefield?

WIFE. No. California.

HUSBAND. Too far to drive.

WIFE. Much too far.

HUSBAND. Why did he go so far away?

WIFE. He was divorced. He lost his job.

HUSBAND. Why were we proud of him?

WIFE. When he was a student. That's when we were proud of him.

HUSBAND. Not anymore.

WIFE. We still love him.

HUSBAND. Love him?

WIFE. You don't stop loving someone, just because they're having...
    problems.

HUSBAND. When do you stop loving them?

WIFE. You don't stop.

HUSBAND. You don't?

WIFE. You shouldn't stop.

HUSBAND. Even if you're not proud of them anymore?

WIFE. Especially if you're not.

HUSBAND. That would be the best time to stop, wouldn't it?

WIFE. That's when they need you the most.

HUSBAND. What can I do for David? I can't do anything for him.

WIFE. We've helped him.

HUSBAND. Did we find him a job?

WIFE. We loaned him some money.

HUSBAND. When is he paying us back?

WIFE. When he can.

HUSBAND *(After a long beat)*. I dream sometimes. I dream.

WIFE. What do you dream?

HUSBAND. I'm walking down the street. People say hello to me.

WIFE. People you know?

HUSBAND. They say hello to me.

WIFE *(Softly)*. People say hello to you.

HUSBAND. I go into a big building. They know me. "Hello." "How are you today?" "How's the family?"

WIFE. Is it your office building? Where you used to work?

HUSBAND. My office building.

WIFE. Do you go to your office?

HUSBAND. I go to my office. Sit down at my desk. There are folders and
    papers on my desk. I look at them.

WIFE. You're back at work.

HUSBAND. I can't read them. The letters are blurry. Too small. *(With
    growing anxiety)* I can't read them. Don't know where I am. Why I'm
    there. What I'm supposed to be doing. Don't know.

WIFE. It's only a dream, dear.

HUSBAND. Don't know. Even when I wake up.

WIFE *(She takes his hand in hers)*. I wish I could make it better for you.

HUSBAND. How long have we been married?

WIFE. Forty-four years. Forty-five in June.

HUSBAND. We wanted to be happy.

WIFE. We were happy.

HUSBAND. I don't remember being happy.

WIFE. We were.

HUSBAND. I don't remember.

WIFE. Our first house—our first home—was a garden apartment in Norwalk.
    A second floor walk-up. We had an electric stove and I left a pot
    on the burner too long. *(She laughs)* I almost burned a hole in the
    kitchen ceiling.

HUSBAND. Norwalk?

WIFE. We didn't have much, but we were happy there.

HUSBAND. When did we stop being happy?

WIFE. We didn't stop.

HUSBAND. Are you happy now?

WIFE. Yes.

HUSBAND. I'm not.

WIFE. That's because of your...problems.

HUSBAND. I think of our lives—sometimes I can remember—sometimes.
    Not everything. Some things.

WIFE. What do you remember?

HUSBAND. I don't remember being happy.

WIFE. We were.

HUSBAND. Molly did things—we didn't want her to do.

WIFE. Yes. There was a time—drugs, the wrong kind of people.

HUSBAND. Sweet little Molly.

WIFE. It wasn't a good time.

HUSBAND. We weren't happy.

WIFE. We weren't happy.

HUSBAND. Did David make us happy?

WIFE. Yes.

HUSBAND. Not anymore.

WIFE. He's still young. I have hope.

HUSBAND *(After a long beat)*. I should have gone to law school.

WIFE. I told you to go.

HUSBAND. You didn't mean it.

WIFE. I did.

HUSBAND. You said it but you didn't mean it.

WIFE. That was so long ago. A million years ago.

HUSBAND. I knew you didn't mean it.

WIFE. Believe me, I—

HUSBAND. You were pregnant. I had to start making money.

WIFE. We would have found a way.

HUSBAND. Law school. That was what I wanted.

WIFE. I know.

HUSBAND. I never went.

WIFE. I really am sorry.

HUSBAND. I started the grind. The grind.

WIFE. You did very well.

HUSBAND. Bees.

WIFE. Bees?

HUSBAND. A bee hive.

WIFE. Is this another dream?

HUSBAND. Drones. Buzzing.

WIFE. I don't know what you mean, dear.

HUSBAND. Building little wax boxes. Millions of them. Over and over. Nameless. Faceless. Drones. Sitting in my office, I could hear the buzzing.

WIFE. You took good care of your family, dear.

HUSBAND *(He stands up)*. I told David once—I remember—he was in high school, I think—I told him not to give up his dreams. Don't give up your dreams!

WIFE. You told him that?

HUSBAND. He said, "I don't have any dreams. I don't know what I want to do with my life."

WIFE. He said that?

HUSBAND. Yes. I remember. I remember. *(Exhausted, he sits down. After a beat)* He had no dreams. Why not?

WIFE. I don't know.

HUSBAND. Our fault?

WIFE. I don't think so.

HUSBAND. Hope not.

WIFE *(After a long silence)*. The first summer we came here, when Molly was just a year old. Oh, that was a wonderful summer!

HUSBAND *(Still exhausted. Softly)*. Tell me.

WIFE. We rented a tiny cabin. It was on the other side of the lake. For a week. One room. A kitchenette. It even had indoor plumbing. And a double bed. We brought a portable crib that converted into a playpen.

HUSBAND. David was a baby?

WIFE. David wasn't born yet. Molly was a year old.

HUSBAND. Sweet Molly.

WIFE. We had picnics in the woods. You took us out on the lake in a rowboat. You rowed very well.

HUSBAND. I did?

WIFE. Yes, you did. And we hiked all over the place. Did a little fishing.

HUSBAND. Did we catch anything?

WIFE. Nothing big enough to eat.

HUSBAND. We spent the summer here?

WIFE. No. We couldn't afford that. Just a week.

HUSBAND. Were we happy?

WIFE. Yes.

HUSBAND. I don't remember that.

WIFE. I wish you could. There were the family parties, too.

HUSBAND. Family?

WIFE. Your mother and father would come. And mine. Your brother Joe
    and his wife. And their kids. My sister, Christine. Thanksgiving.
    Christmas. Everyone would bring a favorite dish. Or a pie. So much
    noise. So much laughter.

HUSBAND. My brother?

WIFE. Joe. His wife, Sharon.

HUSBAND. Joe. Sharon.

WIFE. He died ten—no, twelve years ago. She passed away just two years
    later.

HUSBAND. Passed away. My parents passed away.

WIFE. Yes. Long ago.

HUSBAND. "Passed away" sounds nicer than "died."

WIFE. I guess that's why people say it.

HUSBAND. It isn't nicer because you call it something else.

WIFE. That's true.

HUSBAND. I'm going to be dead soon.

WIFE. Don't say that.

HUSBAND. Why not?

WIFE. You're going to live a long time.

HUSBAND. Do you think I want to?

WIFE. I don't want to lose you.

HUSBAND. Lose me?

WIFE. I love you.

HUSBAND. You've already lost me.

WIFE. I haven't!

HUSBAND. Only little pieces of me are left. I've lost myself.

WIFE. You're still the man I married.

HUSBAND. Not for long.

WIFE. Don't say that.

HUSBAND. I'm not scared to die.

WIFE. Please, don't...

HUSBAND. But I'm afraid to disappear.

WIFE. I'll be here. I'll be with you.

HUSBAND. I'm losing touch...

WIFE. I'll be here.

HUSBAND. With everything.

WIFE. Don't say that!

HUSBAND. You'll be a stranger. Everyone will be.

WIFE *(Beginning to cry).* Please, don't say that.

HUSBAND. I'll be a stranger. I won't know me.

WIFE. You still remember some things.

HUSBAND. Bad things. The good things are disappearing. Like me.

WIFE. I'll help you remember.

HUSBAND. We were proud of David? Good student?

WIFE. That's right.

HUSBAND. I remember his failures. His marriage. Jobs he lost. Nothing else.

WIFE. We were proud...

HUSBAND. You talk about Molly's husband. Children. I remember her taking drugs. Losing. That's all I remember.

WIFE. But she won. Finally, she won.

HUSBAND. Soon, thank God, I won't remember the bad things. But who will I be? Who will I be?

WIFE. My husband. My love.

HUSBAND. Without memories?

WIFE. Don't leave me. Please don't leave me.

HUSBAND. It's not up to me.

WIFE *(She rises, goes to him, embraces him)*. I wish I could do something. I wish, I wish...

HUSBAND. Some memories—old memories—still there.

WIFE *(She releases him, keeps her arm around his shoulder)*. From your childhood?

HUSBAND. Yes.

WIFE. Tell me.

HUSBAND. I'm tired. I'm so tired. I want to sleep.

WIFE. Tell me your memories.

HUSBAND. Growing up, a girl lived next door to us. A couple of years younger than me.

WIFE. You remember her?

HUSBAND. I do.

WIFE. Do you remember her name?

HUSBAND. Mary Anne.

WIFE. Tell me about Mary Anne.

HUSBAND. Very pretty.

WIFE. A pretty little lady?

HUSBAND. No. A "tom-boy"—when women weren't supposed to like sports.

WIFE. A pretty little tom-boy.

HUSBAND. We spent time together. Lots of time.

WIFE. That sounds like a love affair in the making.

HUSBAND *(Yawning)*. I'm tired. I want to sleep.

WIFE. Not just yet. Lean on me. That's it. Tell me more. About Mary Anne.

HUSBAND. Good friends. Close friends. For years.

WIFE. And you can remember her now?

HUSBAND. I wonder what my life would have been if I had married her. Would everything have been different? Better?

WIFE. What do you think?

HUSBAND *(Leans his head against her)*. It was simple then.

WIFE. Yes, it was.

HUSBAND. We were going to win. We knew it.

WIFE. That's what we thought.

HUSBAND. Why do I remember that? The one good thing I remember.

WIFE. I don't know why.

HUSBAND. Mary Anne. Pretty. Wonderful smile. I remember.

WIFE. I'm glad you do.

HUSBAND *(Beginning to fall asleep).* Soon I won't remember. *(Yawns)* What
if I had married Mary Anne?

(He falls asleep, leaning against his WIFE, *in her arms.)*

WIFE. My poor lost boy. I *am* Mary Anne.

(Curtain)

Readers Guide

Please be aware that the Readers Guide may contain spoilers.

"The McKenzie Harvest"

1. When Katherine McKenzie meets Bradley Munson, he asserts that "Rules don't matter....*Breaking* them matters." Katherine responds, "Don't you have to *know* them *before* you break them?" Whose rules has Katherine followed in shaping her artistic and emotional life? How have those rules affected the choices she has made?

2. "Listening"—to music but, more important, to what other people say—is a key element of the story. How is Katherine influenced by listening to her mother? To Amos Greene in Boston—and, later, when he writes to her? To her mentor Simon Levin? To her brother Duncan, and sister Jean Anne? And, of course, to Bradley?

3. Before Katherine and Bradley make love that first time, she pointedly tells him she is not in love with him. Why does she want him to know that? And later, "when the pleasure washed over her, it wasn't about Jeremy or Bradley. She felt that the pleasure was hers, and hers alone." Why is it important for her to feel that way? How does that moment contrast with the last night she spent with Jeremy?

4. When we first meet Katherine, she is dominated by fear. She is a talented concert pianist afraid of audiences, a young woman afraid of her own sexuality, a farm girl afraid of the place where she grew up. By the time she decides to return to Boston, has she resolved some of her fears?

5. She invites Bradley to join her in an effort to promote his music. Do you think he will follow her?

6. Contrast Katherine's attitude toward religion with Duncan's beliefs. What was her mother's attitude toward religion? Why do you think her mother felt that way?

7. Does Katherine finally accept Kansas as her home?

"The Food of Love" and "The Legend of Jean-Paul LeBeau"

1. Compare and contrast the personality and character of three musical virtuosos: Katherine McKenzie, Maximilian Solange and Jean-Paul LeBeau.

2. Music plays a significant role in "The McKenzie Harvest," "The Food of Love" and "The Legend of Jean-Paul LeBeau." Discuss the role of music in each of these stories.

3. Who is the composer of "The Food of Love" and why did she create that piece of music?

4. Why is music such an important element in the religious services of so many faiths?

"The Messenger"

1. Why is the narrator of the story so unhappy?

2. How does the narrator view his relationship to God?

3. Why did Joshua Daniels write the letter to Mrs. Anderson?

4. How does Joshua view his relationship to God?

5. What is his message? Has anyone heard it?

"The Boarding House"

1. Who is Adler and why is he in the boarding house? Who is the landlord?

2. Why is Adler mute? Weak? Impotent?

3. Did the prospect of an afterlife affect the way Adler behaved?

"Goldman the Jeweler"

1. Discuss Goldman the Jeweler's moral code and how it affects his family, his employees, and his business practices.

2. Who has a motive to kill Goldman? The opportunity? The means? Based on the evidence at the crime scene, who do you think is the murderer?

3. What happened to Goldman's stash of cash? What will happen to his "off-the-books" jewelry?

4. Will his killer be caught?

"Final Arrangements"

1. A question for discussion: Is Abel Pritchard a success or a failure—in business—in his emotional life?

2. Why does Abel feel the need to "revisit" the people who mattered most to him—the people he loved?

3. Do you think he finds peace?

"Mary Anne"

1. Do the Wife's memories suggest that the couple loved each other and had a happy marriage?

2. What does the Husband remember about his children? His job? His parents and his brother?

3. What is the Husband's attitude toward death?

4. Why does the Wife urge the Husband to remember?

"The Food of Love and Other Tales of Lovers, Dreamers and Schemers"

1. What is the effect of this collection as a whole—the order, the contrasting styles and formats, the settings, the characters?

2. Compare the endings of several of these tales. Are problems solved, issues resolved? Or are there still questions to be answered, actions to be taken?

3. Compare the way "love" is portrayed in these stories—love between man and wife, parental love, love of power, love of art, love of pleasure, love of God.

4. Considering the collection as a whole, what is the author's view of love? Of life? Of God?

www.ingramcontent.com/pod-product-compliance
Lightning Source LLC
Chambersburg PA
CBHW031333060726
47590CB00007B/2449